GERMAN FOR TRAVELERS
A NOVEL IN 95 LESSONS

NORAH LABINER

COFFEE HOUSE PRESS
MINNEAPOLIS :: 2009

COFFEE HOUSE PRESS books are available to the trade through our primary distributor, Consortium Book Sales & Distribution, www.cbsd.com or (800) 283-3572. For personal orders, catalogs, or other information, write to: info@coffeehousepress.org.

Coffee House Press is a nonprofit literary publishing house. Support from private foundations, corporate giving programs, government programs, and generous individuals helps make the publication of our books possible. We gratefully acknowledge their support in detail in the back of this book.

To you and our many readers around the world,
we send our thanks for your continuing support.

LIBRARY OF CONGRESS CIP INFORMATION
Labiner, Norah, 1967–
German for travelers : a novel in 95 lessons / Norah Labiner. — 1st ed.
p. cm.
ɪᴏᴏᴢɪ ɪɡɪ ɡᴛ̄ᴂ ɪ ɟ6689 ᴐᴐɔ ᴐ (ᴏllɾ ᴘᴐᴘᴂʀ)
ISBN-IO: 1-56689-206-6
1. Family secrets—Fiction.
I. Title.
PS3562.A2328G47 2009
813'.54—DC22
2008052719

PRINTED IN CANADA
1 3 5 7 9 8 6 4 2
FIRST EDITION | FIRST PRINTING

The author gratefully acknowledges the support of the Minnesota State Arts Board and the National Endowment for the Arts.

GERMAN FOR TRAVELERS

The whole thing is planned on the model of an imaginary walk. First comes the dark wood of the authorities (who cannot see the trees), where there is no clear view and it is easy to go astray. Then there is a cavernous defile through which I lead my readers—my specimen dream with its peculiarities, its details, its indiscretions and its bad jokes—and then all at once, the high ground and the open prospect and the question: which way do you want to go?

—Sigmund Freud, 1899

LESSON 1

More and more people travel by train
Immer mehr Leute reisen mit dem Zug

———

Go to Berlin, you really should.

Go to Berlin for the sightseeing; the shopping; the skyscrapers; the buttery *Strudel* and *Schweinefleisch;* the big-boned blondes; the unargumentative streets; the rebuilt ruins; the buried bunker; the film festivals where movie stars meet; the lifelike mannequins and supermodels; the crowded dance clubs; the gay pride parades in summer; the snow in winter; the aquarium and the zoo. Don't forget to see what's left of the Wall.

Visit while the exchange rate is good; while the plums are in season.

You need not know the whole of the language to enjoy your stay. *Bring a coffee, please! And an éclair!* Point to objects. Or pantomime. Mimic raising a cup to indicate that you would like coffee. Or ape eating to show how much pleasure an éclair would bring.

Avoid the complexities of grammar.

The best way to learn is to do; to watch; to practice; to repeat.

Take what you need.

Want what you will.

It all awaits you in Berlin.

LESSON 2

Danke says thank you
Bitte is please

———

Lemon Leopold sat at the edge of the swimming pool.

Her brother, drunk in a deck chair, covered his eyes with his forearm.

She wore a black bikini.

She dangled her bare legs into the water.

She said, "A man walks into a psychiatrist's office. He says 'Doctor, Doctor, I think I'm God.'" She paused. "Have you heard this one?" Lemon said. "The doctor says, 'When did this start?' And the man says, 'Well first I created the sun, then the earth.'"

Ben Leopold did not laugh.

"Did I tell it wrong?" Lemon asked.

She splashed her feet in the water.

There was a script beside her.

She opened it and flipped through the pages.

"I've been working on my English accent," she said.

"Do you want to hear?" she asked.

He looked up at the sky.

The sun continued to shine.

He seemed disappointed.

"What should we do tomorrow?" she asked.

She said that she felt like doing something tomorrow.

Ben looked at his glass.

It was empty.

An airplane flew overhead.

A butterfly hovered over the pool.

Lemon sat reading the script.

"Here," Ben said, "this came for you."

He held a letter.

She rose and went to him.

She took the letter from him.

She studied the envelope.

"Eliza is in Germany," she said.

He said that he had looked at the postmark.

"She's gone to Berlin," he said.

"Why would she go back?" asked Lemon.

Ben closed his eyes.

He said that people often return years later—with familiarity, with nostalgia—to the site of past tragedy. He said something about a study done on the survivors of a terrible plane crash. He used the word *pathology*.

Lemon interrupted him.

"Face it," said Lemon, "El has rotten luck."

She asked her brother, "Do you believe in luck?"

"Please don't get deep," he said.

"This is California," she said.

He said, "What does that mean?"

He said, "I don't know what that means."

She set the letter, unopened, atop the script that she had been reading.

Louisa Leopold, billed as Lemon, was called Lou by her brother; and Lulu in the tabloids; she did not have rotten luck. She had had no particular interest in acting when at twelve she had taken part at her mother's urging in a school production of *The Sound of Music*. Lemon's lovestruck Liesl brought tears to the eyes of those parents and relatives in attendance on opening night. It also just so happened that there was a talent scout in that audience. One thing led to another, and she ended up playing the smart-mouthed daughter on a sitcom for four seasons until at sixteen a growth spurt left her taller than her television father. And she was fired. And the firing of Lemon Leopold, who had grown up before the eyes of America as Sammy Sellars on *Not in My House!* inspired legions of fans to protest, write letters to the network, and take up, in general, the cause of the mistreated young starlet whose height, certainly, was beyond her control. Lemon was happy to leave the show behind and head for the big screen. She displayed (along with full nudity), the critics said—and audiences agreed—remarkable talent and maturity, when at eighteen she played a crack-addicted prostitute in an award-winning film.

Not in My House! was cancelled the season after Lemon's departure.

Lemon, the once-winsome child star, was now at twenty-eight an acclaimed actress.

What were these strange twists of circumstance if not luck?

She flipped through the pages of the script.

"Poor cousin Eliza," she said.

"What's that?" he asked.

"It's my Bette Davis," she said.

"Doesn't it sound like Bette Davis?" she said.

Ben refilled his glass.

He spilled vodka onto the Italian tile of his little sister's patio.

Ben, that is, Dr. Leopold, made thirty-nine seem an impossibly exhausting age.

Lemon's fair hair was clipped short; her white skin, her blue eyes, her fine features—she had been told, and the important magazines devoted to beauty agreed this season—were best offset by boyishly shorn hair. A hat shielded her face from the afternoon sun. Ben was *in crisis*, everyone said. First he had broken it off with his fiancée. And then he abandoned his practice, leaving his patients in the lurch. And what had he done? He had driven across the country to do nothing more soul-searching than lounge around Lemon's house—a Spanish colonial rumored to be haunted by the ghost of Irving Thalberg—drinking vodka.

Lemon didn't mind. It was nice, after all, having her brother around.

In truth, she had never felt as though she knew him.

She felt that she was only now getting to know, to really *know* him.

Ben was *in crisis.*

Lemon was in the movies.

And Eliza was in Germany.

The letter lay unopened.

"Should I open it?" Lemon asked.

"What are you reading?" he asked.

"The script?" she said. "It's futuristic. I think I would have to wear a body suit. I don't know if I want to wear a body suit."

She gave herself a fake punch to her very white and flat stomach.

She said, "A man who thinks he's George Washington goes to see a psychiatrist. He says, 'Doctor, Doctor, tomorrow we'll cross the Delaware and surprise them when they least expect it.' As soon as he's gone, the psychiatrist picks up the phone and says, 'King George, this is Benedict Arnold. I have the plans.'"

Lemon looked at her brother.

A butterfly landed on his hand.

"Let's go to Berlin," she said.

"Really, what's stopping us?" she said.

"Poor Louisa," he said.

"I'm serious," she said. "We could go to Berlin. We aren't *doing* anything; we never *do* anything. We could fly out tonight. I feel like doing something, don't you?"

"What would we do there?" he asked.

"Drink beer," she said. "Eat cake. Follow the breadcrumbs. But I'm off carbs."

Ben said, "Franz baked cakes. Do you remember?"

She said, "I don't remember."

She tried out her English accent.

"It was before me time, Old Bean," she said.

"That's awful," he said.

"Is it funny?" she asked.

"No," he said.

She sighed. "I'm going to have to get a dialect coach."

"Or a space suit," he said.

"What was the best thing that he made?" she asked.

"Black Forest cake," he said.

"With chocolate and cherries?" she said.

He said, "If that's what's in it."

"I thought Mother had you off cake?" he said.

"Don't be so Oedipal," said Lemon.

"What does that mean?" he said.

"Amalie doesn't want me to eat cake," said Lemon. "She doesn't even want me to talk about cake. She says that I'm undisciplined, but I've lost eight pounds."

Ben said, "Two psychiatrists meet on the street. One says to the other, 'You know, I thought I'd been completely analyzed, but yesterday I experienced the most remarkable Freudian slip. I was having dinner with my mother, and I meant to say, "Please pass the butter," but instead I said—'"

"You've told that one before," she said.

Ben asked Lemon for the letter.

Ben and his sister sat beside the swimming pool.

She handed the letter to him.

"I'm fat," she said.

"You're a skeleton," he said.

"We're all *skeletons*," she said.

"You should do more comedy," he said.

"Why," she asked, "would I want to do a crazy thing like that?"

LESSON 3

I come from the United States
Ich komme aus den Vereinigten Staaten

⁓

Eliza woke in the darkness.

It took her a moment to remember.

I am in Germany. I am in a hotel room in Germany.

My name is Eliza Berlin, but what is unstoppably or relentlessly German about me?

What was truly, unstoppably, or relentlessly German about Eliza Berlin?

She went to the window. She opened the curtains.

The city that bore her name stretched forth: wakeful, waiting.

Somewhere below: cakes were being baked; trees and bombs planted; pills taken; dice rolled. People went to work; children went to school.

Eliza's hotel room contained: a bedspread and television. Things that you could fold, hurl out a window, or use to shroud a corpse. Things like soap, toothbrush, pen, pillow, lampshade, and pajamas. Things with weight when they fall, a heft that hurts; insignificant, important, shoe, table, suitcase, glass, book, sock, clock, ring, and key.

On the door: a lock and number.

How do you *exist* in case of emergency?

A sign on the door explained: *how to exit in case of emergency.*

Eliza had returned to Berlin after fifteen years.

She came to hear a story.

She was as strange as any stranger in a strange land.

Where are the bards and balladeers and troubadours?

Where are the irresistible jongleurs?

She came back to the city where she had lost Hart Luther.

Who was Hart Luther?

Hart Luther's death had been a spectacle. Outsized, unforeseen; improbable—

There are certain improbabilities that while implausible are not impossible. Like winning the lottery or surviving a disaster.

Do you agree that distances are not so great as they once seemed?

Remember when the scale on a map was such that the pinch of a fingertip equaled a thousand miles?

What do you need to take with you from one place to the next?

You aren't a hermit crab; you don't carry your home on your back.

You aren't a bird, who flies from branch to branch.

What brought Eliza to Berlin?

Don't say: airplane.

What did Eliza expect to find in Germany?

A city in darkness is romantic.

What is the problem with romance?

Do you remember romance?

Was Eliza beautiful?

Her hair was the color of Coca-Cola.

Her eyes were Hershey's bar brown.

Time is tricky.

And so Eliza came to Berlin.

To hear a story.

To be told an obscure tale of obscenity and evolution.

To hear about dreams, disbelief, and a girl called Elsa Z.

To learn about Dr. Jozef Apfel.

To find and be found by ghosts.

She grew up a world away from Germany.

In America, in the Midwest, where new cars rolled endlessly off the assembly lines, who ever gave a thought to the past?

When she was twenty-one, she felt that Berlin was nothing short of miraculous. Then: she had arrived a bride and left a widow.

Now: there was a Burger King on the Alexanderplatz.

Billboards advertised Coca-Cola.

Placards promoted: *Doctor, Doctor,* a psychological thriller starring Lemon Leopold.

In the November cold birds clustered hungry and dark-winged upon marble monuments.

She closed the curtains.

Eliza fell for fanatics.

She had other faults and failings. Her flaws, to list: she was not methodical, nor neat nor thorough, neither tough nor timid nor truculent, nor intractable. For like so many dark-eyed dreamers, though she seemed brooding and burdened, she was not too grave or very deep. She would always take the easy path over the difficult proposition.

She came to Berlin.

It was, after all, a remarkable city.

Who was Dr. Apfel? Who was Elsa Z.?

Eliza was not ready to hear the story.

Instead she had whiled away her time sightseeing.

She saw such things: the balcony of the Hotel Adlon over which Michael Jackson famously dangled his store-bought baby; the Landwehr Canal where the body of Rosa Luxemburg had floated corset and boot-bare; even found that Kreuzberg café where at three a.m. she and Hart Luther had sat and sipped *Milchkaffee* along with the other insomniacs, with the late-night losers and lovers alike. She strolled around a bit and looked at the mannequins in the shop windows, took a seat on a bench at the zoo; and there before an audience of ring-tailed lemurs, she wrote—pen to paper—a letter.

Dear Lou—
Here I am in Berlin.
How tricky is time?
It was morning. Wasn't it? It was afternoon. It was night.
Outside the drawn curtains rain began to fall.
It is easy to lose track of time in Berlin.

LESSON 4

She bit into the apple
Sie biss in den Apfel

———

Starting out, embarking upon a journey—don't be overwhelmed—you will have many questions. *May I check my bags through to my final destination? Has the flight begun boarding? Excuse me, is this seat taken?* Oh! Simple things—upon arrival—but so basic: *Where might I find a good restaurant? Are the streets safe? Is rain expected? Will this train stop at the next station?*

Be assured: there are answers to all of your questions.

Do not leave luggage unattended; do not accept packages from strangers. Avoid: conspicuous clothing, jewelry, excessive amounts of money and unnecessary credit cards; familiarize yourself with local customs.

Problems may occur, but problems have solutions.

Knowing where—how—when—in what manner—these problems may arise will help you quickly to overcome the occasional troublesome situation.

Don't worry: later you will laugh in recollection.

Take a moment now to consider: *what is my problem?*

What is your problem? Are you anxious? Argumentative? Overeager? Easily led astray? Do you have a sweet tooth? A dark side? An addiction? Are you passive? Aggressive? A people-pleaser? Do you fear contamination, germs, and vermin? Do small confined spaces cause your heart to hurry? How good is your memory? Do you go at things straight on, with resolve, with grim determination and stubborn faith in the future? Or do you linger lamenting backwards and take in without hope the whole of history? Some people have a habit for hunger; others cannot quite quit the past.

Planes depart by the hour.

Purchase a ticket; take a seat.

You have only to close your eyes; no sooner have you arrived.

The first problem faced by travelers to foreign lands is the acclimation to time.

You must do more than reset your watch. You must imagine living in either yesterday or tomorrow. Which will you choose?

LESSON 5

He climbed the ladder
Er ist auf die Leiter gestiegen

Mrs. Marx was reading Freud.

At the window.

Upon a velvet cushion slept a cat, curled.

Awaiting always sunlight.

There was no sunlight.

Not in Berlin.

But there was cake.

And tea in a flowered china cup.

She had woken that morning from a dream with the terrible and childish presumption that something was about to happen. And so forgive her; forgive yourself; as the cat uncurled to paw the windowpane; if she for a moment forgot her own age.

Did the cat want in or out?

Mrs. Marx was—she felt—in some essential way: German.

That tree had such deep roots.

She set the book upon the table.

Lately, she had found herself subject to strange dreams.

She wanted to know the meaning of her dreams.

What if her dreams contained only symbols to replace symbols?

One can always exit in case of emergency.

Existence is more difficult.

Upon the low table—the flowered cup, a piece of blue notepaper.
She took up her pen. Upon the blue paper—
She drew a bird. She drew another bird. Look—
Like the doves in the plum trees.
The cat was curious.
She looked at her teacup.
She drew a spoon.
She stirred milk into her tea.
Having imagined the spoon, it became real.
Or perhaps a spoon had been upon the table all the while, set
atop a Dresden saucer.
It could have happened like that.
The proof of a dream may rest in its very improbability.
For what one dreams is always possible.
She wore a string of pearls.
And was dressed rather elegantly in dove gray.
As though expecting a visitor.
The afternoon was gray.
Her book fell—abruptly—from the table to the floor.
Mrs. Anna Marx, née Apfel, drank her tea.
She had such dreams. By night they assailed her.
She dreamed of two figures flying across a dark sky.
Against a backdrop of cathedrals and grinning gargoyles.
Up higher and higher they flew.
Until the whole of the sky was enveloped in a black cape.
In black ink.
Into one word that she could not read or understand.
And then—like all dreamers—she woke.
She was searching for that word.
A girl in the next apartment was practicing scales on the piano.

LESSON 6

I'm sure a solution will be found
Es wird sich sicher eine Lösung finden

⁓

Dr. Apfel penned in black ink the date on the page set before him: *Berlin, August 1925.* He continued in his careful cryptic script: *A Fragmentary Analysis of*—he paused; outside the open window—*the Case*—in the garden Tulla plucked black plums—*of Elsa Z.* His dog slept, dreams blissfully unquestioned, stretched out on the wooden floor. Tulla overfilled her basket, and Anna was laughing as she scrambled on the stone path to collect fallen fruit. He could not see from his desk Madame Madeline; her back to him, she sat obscured by a sunshade.

Dr. Apfel crossed out the word *Fragmentary.*

Tulla chided: *Anna, keep out of the roses!*

The doctor wrote: *The events of this narrative begin in October 1919, when Herr and Frau Z. consulted me regarding the condition of their daughter.*

He worked, seated in his bedraggled desk chair; amid the comfortable disarray of his office: the low tea table cluttered with papers, with confidences, correspondence, letters, notes, arguments that fluttered in the wind and fell to the floor. On shelves and in cases crowding the walls crammed were his collections: statuettes of Greek gods and terra-cotta figurines; insects preserved in amber; amulets; erotes; scarabs; carved wooden boxes containing coins, buttons, engraved beads, teeth, and talismen; Mycenaean jars, marbles, and Aegean antiquities; Egyptian shabtis; jade elephants; a painted plaster parrot; books; candle holders; bronze bookends lying in the shape of sleeping dogs; magnifying glasses; microscopes; mirrors; medicines; magnets; calipers; fat little ivory Buddhas and lean bodhisattvas; Russian dolls that opened one from the next ever smaller; scissors; poetry volumes, glue pots; page knives, letter openers; vials; violets in a glass vase. His desk no less occupied: a plate with the remains of a lemon tart; a teacup; a spoon set crosswise upon saucer; pens; pipes; ink; the dutiful old Kenzler *Schreibmaschine* with a page rolled in its carriage.

There were two rooms proper to the doctor's office in his grand gloomy house. And behind a conspicuously closed door—with key resting unturned in its lock—was the inner room—small and quiet—where the doctor saw his patients.

Anna, the little daughter of Dr. Apfel and his second wife, Madeline, chased after the black plums calling out to demand, but sweetly and tart with laughter: *Maman! Aidez-moi!* Madeline Apfel, who sat writing a letter to her faraway stepson Franz on that summer day while Anna trampled the peppermint and thyme, was French, and the maids called her Madame rather than Frau. Madame in marriage had abandoned Paris for Berlin. Despite her elegance, her low musical voice and *soi-disant* loneliness, Madeline, with her black dresses, her dark hair and pale skin, was not haughty, nor aloof, nor unkind. The two girls, Tulla and Dolfi, kept in the Apfel's employment were never once beaten. Tulla bossed. And shy Dolfi preferred to stay hidden in the kitchen. She cooked meals for the family, but her talent, her passion, was for baking. Her jam tarts were nothing short of heartbreaking. It seemed wrong to cleave the crust with a common fork; and yet how could one not? The cat who lived in the kitchen was called Cake. Anna kept also a brown kitten called Kartoffel.

When Madeline played the piano, Anna sat on the sofa turning the pages of a picture book; she dressed her doll; or dangled loops of string to the awaiting paws of her dear little Potato. Anna liked it best when Maman with her black hair pinned up played songs and sang aloud in English: *Yes, We Have No Bananas!* Tulla and Dolfi threw the ball back and forth to Anna in the garden when the weather was fine.

Dr. Apfel's days teemed with neurotics, with sadists and masochists and fetishists, with chronophiles and kleptomaniacs, with obsessives and perverts and prevaricators. He treated a man who dreamed nightly that he was being consumed by rats. And he saw a woman crazed with cleanliness who nevertheless longed to devour dirt. During the war, it had humbled the doctor to accept payment in the form of barter. He had taken food packages, and British, American, and Swiss currency. Tulla made deals and navigated the mysteries of the black market. She learned soldier's slang and taught it to wide-eyed Dolfi: turnip jam was *hero's butter* or *axle grease.* The boys ate *straw and mud:* yellow peas with sauerkraut; spooned up *shrapnel soup:* what a mealy pea and bean broth; and suffered *barbed wire:* dried vegetables and beans; but preferred best of all to dine upon purloined British rations, most especially boiled bully beef straight out of the tin. Milk, meat, soap, fuel, and paper were scarce. Dolfi worked miracles with sawdust-thickened ersatz bread and artificial beer. Anna was born into the midst of it in 1915, a determined Parisian from her first delicate gurgle: *G-G-uerre!*

Oh, but after the Great War! Dolfi concocted cakes. She turned out *Torten* and tarts. She put up jam, jellies, and stewed fruit in summer. Lime honey and lingonberry curd; strawberry marmalade; peach, plum, and pear preserves lined the pantry shelves. She filled jars with candied cherries and blushing green lady apples in syrup. Her molasses-dark gingerbread burned the tongue with a delicious sting.

Her rolled doughnuts she called *Berliners,* but Tulla said *Bismarcks.* Dolfi cracked eggs and creamed butter. She pulled the strings of her apron in an x across her back and tied them tightly around her slim waist in a bow. She sang while mixing coffee, chocolate, and brandy for her Moroccan cake. She folded the melted chocolate into a bowl of whipped heavy cream. Madame called it *gâteau russe,* and found to her delight that it was not unlike a French *dacquoise.* Tulla sat in the kitchen with her sewing bag while her friend shelled and sifted. Tulla told stories. Dolfi listened as she chopped hazelnuts. She pared and paused and pondered. Tulla told a story about a boy who had been so in love with her that he had stood outside her window every night for a year. The two cats slept near the warmth of the oven. And Dolfi believed and disbelieved as the spoon turned in the bowl.

As the August afternoon turned from sun to shadow, Tulla collected Anna, and Anna collected the basket of plums, and Madame pronounced that there was a chill—yes, yes, do you feel it? In the air. At his desk, among his relics, remainders, and reminders, the doctor wrote: *What have I wordlessly awaited if not the passage of time? Did I hope for understanding and insight through memory? Or did I desire the relief of forgetting her? Just as the difficult patient clings with jealous resolve to the satisfaction of his own pain, so have I held on to my failure for fear of something worse.*

Tulla came into the doctor's office later that evening and picked up the papers, which fell, which had fallen to the floor, scattered and out of sequence on the tapestry rug. She arranged them by number: one, two, three. She unfastened the sash and pulled closed the curtains.

LESSON 7

Do you want to go to the museum?
Hast du Lust, ins Museum zu gehen?

———

The doctor's grand Gothic house is standing to this day; and though it has long been emptied of the presence of his family, though they no longer inhabit the drafty rooms or sit in the sun-shadowed garden, something of them remains. Think about those faces fossilized in and onto the walls of Pompeii, preserved in stone just at the moment of oblivion; and then think about Jozef Apfel's lovely second wife, his son Franz, and little daughter Anna. Each one of them—father, mother, brother, sister—believed in the vicissitudes of fate. How else were they to explain the curious turns of their fortune? What mother was more elegant than Madame Madeline? What father stood quite so fine and upstanding, so intelligent, astute, and morally accurate as the good doctor? Summers they spent at the seaside. Winter evenings were whiled away over cups and spoons and saucers. The tea was hot; the cream was cold. The pots in the kitchen shined with well-scrubbed superiority. There were no dogs more diligent, nor clocks less critical than theirs.

Even the books on their shelves told tales better than those found in other tomes.

Dr. Jozef Apfel, psychoanalyst and author of the triangular seduction theory, treated those in his city suffering from visions, vices, obsession, and delusion. He helped unhappy brides and bashful grooms—now mantel-confined as antiques in fading wedding photos—to find their way in the world. The world! Berlin between the wars was a ravaged metropolis—a twentieth-century head bolted crudely in Frankenstein fashion to the body of a Visigoth—or was it the other way around? Limb-lost soldiers, streetwalkers, bathhouse boys, Dadaists, and dilettantes drank absinthe by the teacup. There were assassinations, strikes, and riots. *Polizei* chased after thieves. In the music halls *das Proletariat* danced to Kurt Weill's *Singspiel.* And Professor Einstein's lectures were packed with paparazzi. Girls swooned in the cinema at the sight of *The Sheik.* In picture postcards of that bygone time ladies in fur jackets walk arm in arm along neat lime tree-lined esplanades with gentlemen in homburg hats. In Dr. Apfel's office upon the horsehair sofa draped with Persian blankets patients confessed secrets.

Behind the doctor's house there was a garden.

Around the garden there was a stone wall.

Roses climbed the wall and gate.

And though this was a long time ago—

The plum trees. The roses—

The garden, the gate, the wall—remain now as then.

Dr. Apfel was and is and remains so, in that way that citizens of eternity claim the right to use all verb tenses regardless of temporal relevance—despite his current and ongoing corporeal lack—the great-grandfather of Eliza Berlin, Lemon and Ben Leopold.

LESSON 8

To manufacture steel you need iron
Zur Herstellung von Stahl wird Eisen benötigt

⸻

"Read it out loud," Lemon said.

Ben opened the envelope.

The letter was written in black ink on blue hotel stationery.

The afternoon was unbearably peaceful.

California was slipping into the Pacific Ocean.

Lemon slipped down from the pool's edge into the water.

Ben tried to decipher Eliza's downward-slanting hand, cursive lapsing into script.

Dear Lou—read Ben.

Here I am in Berlin.

Lemon swam.

Ben continued reading—*Where all the clocks tick the wrong time.*

"I can't make out the next part," he said.

"Her handwriting is impossible," said Lemon.

Ben said that it wasn't the handwriting, but that the ink had run.

Travel is so easy these days. I packed my bag. I purchased my ticket. First you depart and then you arrive. Last week I received a letter from a woman who says that she is our long-lost great-aunt. That she is Anna Apfel, our grandfather's younger sister. And has decided after all these years and years that she wants to tell a story about—

He skipped ahead.

21

Have you heard of a girl called Elsa Z.?

He finished reading the letter.

Lemon climbed out of the pool.

She lay flat on her back and stared up at the sky.

Lemon said that maybe it was time for her to learn about their family history.

Ben said that a *family history* is really just a case study in repetitive neurotic behavior.

He said, "Think of a family as a machine."

"A machine?" she said.

"Like a dishwasher? A typewriter? Or a robot?" she said.

"A train," he said, "running down a track—each generation destined to run the same course, doomed to make the same mistakes again and again."

"God, you're a lousy drunk," she said.

Lemon asked, "Who is Elsa Z.?"

Ben asked her if she was really going to Berlin.

He said something about *codependency.*

He said something about Lemon *enabling* Eliza's erratic behavior.

Lemon toweled dry her hair.

She said, "I wish that I could watch the past like a movie and see what really happened."

LESSON 9

You have to peel the orange before you can eat it
Bevor du die Orange isst, musste du sie schälen

———

The story started, if you can believe it, with the groom's mother. Dorothy Leopold, née Munch, who was called *Dot* by the girls and *Munchkin* by her silver-haired imposingly jocular husband, Jack, whispered it to her husband's sister while the bridesmaids in tomato-red chiffon, clutching their bouquets of baby's breath and carnations, waited outside the chapel on their dyed-to-match tomato-red winklepicker heels. The flower girl, who was in the opinion of some a little too old for the job, proceeded down the aisle.

Amy said no, the first time, whispered Dot.

You don't say, her sister-in-law, Mimi Schecter, murmured in return.

Outside in the courtyard of Temple Beth El, the first June roses were just in bloom, while the full lilacs bent heavy with blossom. But it was not the sudden and early heat wave that surprised the guests on that Sunday afternoon in Detroit in 1961; there came a moment when the organist continued to play, and the friends and family assembled for the wedding of Dr. Mitchell Leopold and Amalie Apfel thought that the bride and groom might never appear.

Mimi clasped her hands on her pocketbook and half-turned in her seat to watch the bridesmaids enter arm in arm with the groomsmen. Dot thought that it was a darling story, and she wouldn't have told it if it had reflected badly on her son. It was sweet, that's all. And by the time the six bridesmaids in red and six groomsmen in white dinner jackets and black trousers with sateen bellhop piping down the side seam, in shoes ever so shiny and black, began to take their slow walk, the story made it one row back from Mimi Schecter by way of her daughter, Joan, who told it to her date, Hillel Brightman, who was tickling her knees beneath her flounced taffeta skirt while the organist played the wedding march.

Two hundred guests in the chapel turned in their seats, their eyes fixed on the doorway. Four hundred damp hands tried to alleviate or relieve themselves of dampness; ladies and girls folded their programs and fluttered fanwise; men wiped their palms on handkerchiefs and in the case of young men and boys, on their good trousers. The rabbi coughed. The cantor cleared his throat. Hillel Brightman's fingers roamed incautiously up around Joan Schecter's garter. The bridesmaids held their wilting bouquets. The groomsmen, the worst off, unabashedly perspired—sweating—in suits of summer-weight wool. Bald heads shone under velvet yarmulkes. Petra Apfel, the flower girl, having emptied her basket row by row of carnations, slipped into a seat in the front row next to her parents, who were also the parents of the bride. It had been the bride's idea not to walk down the aisle on the arm of her father. She and her new husband would enter the chapel and walk together; yes, it was a bit untraditional, but Dot Leopold had endorsed it as a lovely, albeit socialist, metaphor for a couple of dear kids madly in love. And besides—to tell the truth—no one knew what the bride's father was going to do next. And just when all seemed lost, just when Joan Schecter whispered the story to her younger sister, Fran, who tried to tell her date, Sam, who showed not only no interest in the story but no interest in the girl telling it and gave her an admonishing frown, just when the organist was about to give up hope, the bride and groom entered the doorway.

Amalie Apfel, on the arm of her soon-to-be husband, appeared on that very hot wedding day in a snow-white strapless gown with an exceptionally fitted satin bodice that clung reverently and displayed with aid of bone inlay and bust darts the exquisite shape of her snow-white bust tapering down to her slim waist to then blossom about the hips into a skirt composed of layer upon layer of tulle, softly blooming, to a three-quarter length, so that her legs in seamed stockings could be seen leading with ever so much utilitarian grace to her high-arched feet in white satin chisel-toe stiletto heels.

There was a gentle sigh, *Ahh,* from the audience.

The bride held, in hands white-gloved to the wrist, her bouquet of roses.

A short veil—brushing her bare shoulders and affixed by means of pins to her fair hair, which was pulled back at the nape of the neck into a simple rolled chignon—obscured her face.

Was she beautiful? Oh yes, all would agree.

And the groom? He was handsome?

He linked his arm through his bride's own without damaging the light of her entrance. He accomplished this task with intrepid skill. And although he wore a uniform identical to that of his groomsmen—white dinner jacket, white shirt, black bow tie, and black trousers—he possessed an aura of superiority. The tallest of the brigade, with broad shoulders and wavy chestnut-colored hair, he carried himself with an authoritative affability that he had inherited from his doting parents, Jack and Dot, the latter of whom pressed a hankie to her teary eyes.

Mitchell Leopold ushered Amalie Apfel to the wedding canopy.

Those among the friends and family seated in the temple on that June day who had heard the story waited with more anticipation than one normally felt at the wedding of two exceptional young people. It was rumored that the bride might say *no.* It was perhaps not the intention of the groom's mother when she told the story to her sister-in-law, to cast the finality of the wedding contract into doubt. She had a staff of caterers in the temple kitchen attending to roasted chicken breasts and rice, to champagne, and to placecards to ensure orderly tablemates and to tables being arranged exactly per her exacting specifications. She had a band setting up and unpacking their instruments. Dot Leopold, in an ornate mother-of-the-groom dress of crystal-blue satin brocade, with a scoop neck, seamed waist, gathered skirt flowing into wedge-shaped panels, and short but modest sleeves, had no doubt—despite the story—that not only the marriage, but the wedding as well, would be a success.

The rabbi orated. The groomsmen tried to heed the advance directives of Dot Leopold: *no hands in pockets, no neck scratching, no slouching or sneezing, and absolutely no scene stealing.* The matron of honor glowed with damp affection. The bridesmaids—except for the last—stood statue-still. And she, the bride's sister, behaved very badly. She rolled her eyes and tugged rather conspicuously adjusting her strapless bodice. She shifted on her pointy high-heeled shoes. Samuel Berlin, who had been lured into the blind date with Joan Schecter's little sister, Fran, by his friend Hillel Brightman, enjoyed watching the fidgeting antics of this bridesmaid. Hedy Apfel, age sixteen, the last in the row of six girls in uncomfortable red dresses, resembled, she had been told, Grace Kelly; but she didn't let it go to her head. And Sam himself had not gone unnoticed by the audience. He was remarkable for his darkness—and he was looked at—that is, *studied*—with apprehension, curiosity, and appreciation.

The story worked its way back aisle by carnation strewn aisle. In the front row, Margot Apfel, mother of Amalie, Hedy, and Petra, of bride, maid, and flower girl, in a elegant black dress that she had herself sewn from a picture in one of Hedy's Hollywood gossip magazines, knew the story without having to hear it. Many of those on the groom's teeming guest list thought it inappropriate for Mrs. Apfel, who looked a good deal like Rita Hayworth, to wear black, despite the flattering simplicity of the princess lines of her *crêpe de Chine* shift with wide shoulder straps, with a square neckline and arms trimmed in a thick band of black taffeta, with its two bejeweled rhinestone buttons as accents in a jumper style. Her arms were bare. She wore a black hat up under which her fair hair was pinned. And at her side her husband, Franz, as the bride and groom stood before the rabbi, stared up at the ceiling. Only Petra, wearing a tomato-red dress with short balloon-full sleeves, with her elbows on her knees and her heart-shaped face tilted up upon her gloved palms, followed her father's gaze. He saw a monarch butterfly, orange and black, fluttering, searching for escape.

Would the bride say *no?* Would dreams and hopes be dashed? Do all of the lovely Apfel girls resemble Hollywood starlets? And is the father, really, well, you know—*loony?* Mrs. Linda Ziegler, the plump young second wife of a dentist, heard the story and the questions it had accumulated as it drifted past her. Twelve-year-old Bobby Milgrom, a distant cousin of the groom, felt the story pass by him en route to his older sister, Beverly, who caught the end of it and whispered it to her younger sister, Tilly, who out of sheer vanity wasn't wearing her eyeglasses and so squinted at the bride while being fed details by their mother Ellen on her left side and by her sister on her right. Beverly described the bride's dress. Ellen asked if it was true that the bride's father wasn't quite all *there?* Neither girl knew the answer. The butterfly found an open window and flew out into the impossibly hot afternoon, where the last lilacs during the course of the wedding ceremony would go from purple to brown to scatter on the scorched grass of the garden walkway.

The bride said she would. And the groom said he did. And perhaps there was a bit of disappointment among the more dramatically inclined guests, who wouldn't have minded seeing a pretty bride gathering up her snow-white skirts, her snow-white bosom heaving in strapless bodice, hurling her bouquet and running, for mysteriously exigent reasons, out of the temple. But this did not happen. And the more romantic guests were happy indeed. Another young couple starting out in life. The rabbi placed before the groom the wineglass wrapped in a linen napkin. Broad-haired and chestnut-shouldered Mitchell Leopold brought down his foot. And everybody cheered. And everyone clapped. *Hooray!* Well, almost everyone. Everyone on the groom's side cheered. Diminutive Dot Leopold (how could she have given birth to the big, strapping groom?) in her crystal-blue dress and high-heeled shoes, which elevated her to the height of exactly five-feet-no-inches tall, cheered. As did her husband, Jack. *Hooray!* Joan Schecter emitted a squeal of admixed protestation and delight as her date worked his hand up her skirt. Hillel Brightman cheered because the ceremony was over and he wanted a cigarette. Mimi Schecter cheered because both of her daughters had dates. Bobby Milgrom cheered because he was twelve years old. Tilly Milgrom cheered even though she could only make out the blurry shapes of distant figures in black and white and tomato-red. Linda Ziegler cheered because she was a newlywed herself. Dr. Ziegler cheered because he was the groom's dentist. Beverly Milgrom cheered because, unlike her sister, she didn't need glasses. The mother of the bride remained silent. The father of the bride yelled *hooray*. The butterfly had escaped. Petra, the flower girl, said very quietly *hooray* and was embarrassed by the sound of her tiny voice. The dark young man who was the unhappy date of Fran Schecter said *hooray* in a weary and ironic tone. The rabbi presented the married couple to their guests. *Hooray.* Dr. & Mrs. Mitchell Leopold. The veil was lifted. The beautiful bride was kissed by the handsome groom. *Hooray.* Dr. & Mrs. Leopold walked arm in arm down the aisle to exit, and the wedding party followed, and then eventually row by row, at first orderly and then a bit more disorderly, the congregation vacated from first to back rows, from parents of the happy couple to shy girls and stragglers. As she walked with her husband out of the chapel, all could see the beautiful face of Amalie Apfel Leopold divested of veil. A strand or two of her hair fell loose of her chignon. Her pale-pink lips—so nuptially kissed—smiled graciously. And it was impossible to tell, really, that her blue eyes, which had been expertly attended to with white powder to cover dark circles, had been crying all morning.

In the back row Betsy Winkler whispered to Eloise Spiegel the story she had just heard, *The first time Mitch asked Amy to marry him, he gave her a diamond ring, and she said no. The second time he asked her to marry him, he gave her pearl earrings, and she said no. The third time he asked her to marry him, he bet her that he could run faster than she could. They raced in the park. The third time Mitch asked Amy to marry him, she had to say yes because they raced and he won fair and square.*

Betsy watched the bride and groom leave the chapel.

God, that's sweet, said Eloise, raising a handkerchief to her teary eyes. *I wish that would happen to me.*

LESSON 10

Rubber is elastic
Gummi ist elastisch

———

How good is your memory?

Do you recall Hedy barefoot in a tomato-red tomato-shaped dress? How her shoes were too tight in the heel and pinched her toes? She slipped them off during dinner while the guests feasted on roasted chicken and rice. And for dessert? There awaited almond cookies, plum tarts and iced petits fours, opera creams and chocolates on a silver tray; heaps of fruit heaped up: melon scooped into imperious balls, fat strawberries, black cherries on the stem, clusters of grapes, a riot of raspberries; and at the end of the sweets table stood the wedding cake itself, *herself,* a four-tiered blue-rose bedecked marvel of confectionary architecture presided over by a tiny marzipan bride and groom, who looked, everyone agreed, eerily like the real Dr. & Mrs. Leopold.

Attention, attention!

Two hundred spoons chimed *clink, clink, clink,* against two hundred china cups.

It's always funny when they—

Neither bride nor groom, not Mrs. Amalie née Apfel nor Dr. Mitchell Leopold smashed—no, no, they absolutely did not *smoosh*—cake into the face of the other.

Did you know—?

That Amy said *no* twice before saying *yes* once.

Did you get a look at—?

The groom's sister in her matronly matron-of-honor gown? Mrs. Suzanne Elk, née Leopold, who was called Susie by the girls and Sooz by her portly husband, Gerald, is best described in the connotation of fruit as being *apple-* rather than *pear-shaped*.

Did you see—?

How sixteen-year-old Hedy didn't make a grab—not a reach!— for the bride's bouquet when it was tossed right to her? Hedy let the bouquet drop at her feet. And Petra, just eleven, reached down and picked it up. She tried to hand it over to Hedy—who would not take the thing. Poor Amy! What was she to do about her impossible sisters? Amy was the oldest of the one, two, three Apfel girls— absolutely ancient—all of twenty years, in her wedding white gown.

Who served dinner at Dr. & Mrs. Mitchell Leopold's wedding reception?

Black women in black uniforms with white collars, in black stockings and white aprons.

Was there a bar?

Champagne flowed—popped were corks but no corked pops— for the toasts. There was no booze; no spiking; no tippling; no drunk-and-disorderlying. Many full flutes, or nearly so, went flat, abandoned for sweeter tastes.

About that cake—?

The bride and groom posed, sharing the knife, for the photographer, and hand over hand plunged the blade into the grand vanilla-and-lemon cream wedding cake. Then the knife was given to a woman in a black dress with white apron. And she began to carve up the cake. Girls stood first in line, demurely, shyly, not knowing what to do with their hands while waiting to receive the plate. Then the boys, with much jostling, fist making, fart noising and arm punching. The cake diminished, slivered and slabbed, set upon plates and served to the grown-ups who waited at their tables to plunge forks into frosting and proclaim à la mode vox populi: *delicious!*

What happened to the parents of the bride?

Franz and Margot Apfel slipped away before the cutting of the cake, which had been baked, constructed lovingly, maddeningly, tier by tier, by the father of the bride himself. Doors, windows, fire escapes, kitchens, alley exits, and likewise suitable or secret means of disappearance never went unnoticed by Herr and Frau Apfel.

And no one saw them leave?

Hedy noticed. She was trying in vain to get drunk. She drank her flute of champagne and then finished off those of her nontippling tablemates. She saw her parents heading toward the kitchen, and she knew that soon they would pass through the swinging doors and then out the back way—outside—and they would be gone. Petra noticed Hedy noticing. Petra, stuck at the kiddy table where a legion of tiny girls—cousins, nieces, daughters—looked vengefully at her for having usurped the coveted role of flower girl, *saw* Hedy *see* their parents disappear. A little girl poked her in the arm with a fork and had the nerve to pretend it was an accident. Petra stood up and straightened her tomato-red dress—she wanted to leave—when just a gaggle of the groom's great-aunts, who thought she was utterly darling, immediately seized upon, grabbed, and cooed over her. What an adorable child! It is difficult to believe that people used to do such things: her cheeks were pinched by innumerable fingers.

Who invited Samuel Berlin?

Hillel Brightman and Joan Schecter fixed him up with Joan's younger sister, Fran.

What about Hedy?

She was dramatic. She had her heart set on disaster. She had a world-weary beauty, a wide-eyed unwilling *Weltschmerz*. Maybe she would be an actress. Maybe one day she would go to Hollywood. She loved the movies. She hated her name. Hedwig Apfel? It was far too German. It lacked poetry. It wanted for romance. Oh, to have a name with a hard anglicized *G*-sounding *J*. Like Jane Eyre or Jennifer Jones. To be or not to be Shakespearean: a tragic Juliet! Why not the regal euphony, the elegance of Elizabeth or Eleanor? Anything but Hedwig! Oh, for the Gallic glamour of Jeanne d'Arc, the maid of Orleans!—Oh, to have a name like Genevieve! To be Napoleon's Josephine or de Sade's Justine or Heathcliff's haunted Catherine wandering the moors! *Wuthering Heights* was Hedy's favorite book.

What about Fran Schecter, you know, Samuel Berlin's date?

The matchup of the brooding Samuel Berlin and bespectacled Fran Schecter never took flame. Fran's real love ran deep for dogs. Ask her anything at all about those fuzzy-wuzzy loveadubdubs of the four-footed tail-wagging variety, and she would answer. She had a part-time job after school working in Dr. Leopold's veterinary office. She wanted to be a dog breeder. Joan, her older sister, always giggled at the mention of *dog breeding*.

So what did Sam do?

Fran had a caramel-colored cocker spaniel called Queenie, who could do all manner of tricks: catch, jump, sit, stay, speak, shake a paw, and heel. Joan had her stockinged foot under the table in Hillel's lap. Samuel Berlin thought about calling it quits. He saw the

33

bride's parents sneak out the back way. He saw at a nearby table Hedy Apfel drinking too much champagne. He did not notice that Petra, at the kiddy table, *noticed* him *noticing* Hedy *notice* her parents' departure. The third couple sitting with Sam and Fran, with Joan and Hilly, was made up of a friend of the groom's, an irritating young man named Delmore Brown (formerly Braunstein), and his date, a girl he introduced simply as Barb. Well as it happened, Delmore too loved dogs, and he engaged Fran in an entirely canine discussion. Poor Barb tried to make eyes at Hillel, who was otherwise engaged with Joan's delicately lavender-colored foot; so Barb turned her attention to Sam, and finally, when he wouldn't return her affections, she waited for the wedding cake.

Poor Barb!

Yes, poor Barb indeed. What happened to her? Del Braunstein Brown chatted up the underage Fran all evening and then when he took Barb home, he tried to get fresh with her in the car. What an absolute jerk! Don't worry—Barb was pretty and petite. She had a slim waist and generous hips. You can imagine that even though this night in particular was unhappy for her, she went on to have a happy life. She was more fruitfully pear- than apple-inclined, hips to bustwise.

Oh, Hedy!

Sam rose from his seat at the table. He went to Hedy; Hedy in her ill-fitting red dress; he stood behind her and said into her ear, over her bare shoulder—he whispered—*My name is Samuel Berlin, but there is nothing particularly German about me.*

God but it was hot—

that day. It was forty years in the desert hot. It was golden calf is melting hot. It was Tomb of the Patriarchs hot. It was hot enough to

34

fry an egg hot. It was girls with round bare arms hot. It was if this is June can you imagine July? hot. It was boys with ties rakishly askew like junior G-men hot. It was the band in shirtsleeves and suspenders hot. It was hot enough for you? hot. It was wedding programs folded and used as fans for fanning flushed faces hot. It was in the kitchen women in black dresses and white aprons pausing between plates to stand before the opened windows hot. It was I saw Jerry Lewis at the Copa in '57 and no one was hotter hot. It was it's not the heat it's the humidity hot. It was by the Rivers of Babylon hot. It was seven ill-favored and lean kine eating up seven well-favored and fatfleshed kine hot. It was and so Pharaoh awoke hot.

What happened after?

After the dancing, after the last plates and coffee cups were cleared away, when the tablecloths were heaped, when the band packed up their instruments, when the drummer left with one of the bridesmaids on his arm, when the cake was divided up and the sweets were portioned out, when the flowers and centerpieces were given preferentially to preferred guests by Dot Leopold, after all this; the bride and groom, changed into traveling clothes, and they, divested of their black and white, headed off that very night on their honeymoon.

LESSON 11

In winter the nights are longer than in summer
Im Winter sind die Nächte länger als im Sommer

⁓

Eliza stood before the address she had memorized. On the Charlottenstrasse—

The place was not what she had imagined.

Place seldom was as she imagined it.

The apartment building was modern, bright steel and glass.

In Germany no one wants to be part of the past.

Everyone is looking to the future.

She traveled by the underground from the station at the Zoologischer Garten. On the nearby Friedrichstrasse were luxury shops and department stores.

The Sony cinema on the Potsdamer Platz was showing Lemon Leopold's latest film.

Tourists strolled arm in arm.

A skinhead in boots with white laces turned up his leather collar against the rain.

Around the corner there was a bakery.

The street smelled of chocolate and cherries.

Schwarzwälder Kirschtorte.

Black Forest cake.

It was hard for her to think about the word *chocolate* as having anything to do with actual *chocolate*. It was hard to think about what happens in the darkest darkness of forests.

How do you reconcile the difference between *a thing* and *the idea* of that thing?

Between *a word* and what that word *represents*.

Between *a place* and *the idea* of a place.

How different is *chocolate* from *Schokolade?*

She saw a piece of rain-sogged paper on the sidewalk before her.

Eliza was in the habit of collecting what other people had discarded.

She inherited from her father a penchant, though perhaps less literal, for preservation. He owned a run-down antique shop. She grew up a world away from Germany.

Father's shop was called without apostrophe or explanation: Berlin.

In Father's shop all the clocks ticked the wrong time.

She found such treasures: marbles, charms, grime-green foreign coins, rings, buttons, books with torn pages, and moldering magazines still bright with pictures of faraway places.

Now she was in a faraway place.

Words replace things.

Names replace people.

Father was Sam. Mother was Hedy.

Mother was dead; Father, gloomy.

Mother's sister was Petra.

And after Mother died, Petra took care of Father and Eliza.

Everything in their house was twice-abandoned—slightly elegant, partly broken, mostly dilapidated, marked by misuse—and mythical Great-grandfather was no exception.

She knew his face from a silver-framed photograph on the wall.

When she was a child, she thought it was a photograph of God.

He was stern and solemn-seeming.

He looked down on the family quizzically, but without reproach.

He presided from his picture frame against the peeling floral wallpaper; he watched over the ponderously heavy mahogany table with its embroidered cloth, the chipped china, the mismatched brass candlesticks. He saw the father; the almost mother; the child.

He seemed at any moment ready to pronounce his judgment—

And then she grew; she learned; she understood that he was her mother's grandfather.

He was important. He was Dr. Jozef Apfel.

Eliza knew his face from photographs on book jackets.

And though she felt silly for having once thought he was God, she still feared in some small but *important* way, his judgment.

The day was dark.

The city gloomy.

She picked up the paper. She folded and put it in her pocket.

It was only a note, a scribble, something fallen, or that a child had lost.

Wet with rain—the words, ink on paper—had run.

She walked.

And turned toward the Unter den Linden.

What is there to do on a dark day in a gloomy city but wander?

It is said that ghosts stroll the promenades.

Why, at dusk one can sometimes make out the specter of Cartaphilus who having witnessed Christ's death was cursed to walk the world for eternity—

He had been seen lonely and loitering about the cinema.

Look! Isn't that Martin Luther asleep on a park bench?

And there—Marlene Dietrich, mournful in marabou, struggles to open her umbrella?

Eliza imagined that Hart Luther was a ghost walking beside her.

Everything ends eventually, but is time spent in retrospect—in retrospection—ever lost or wasted?

LESSON 12

Terrorists attempt to achieve their political aims
by means of violence
*Terroristen versuchen, ihre politischen Ideen mit
Gewalt durchzusetzen*

⸺

At an upper window, a hand drew back a curtain.

LESSON 13

The piano won't go through the door
Das Klavier geht nicht durch die Tür

———

Who was Hart Luther?

A first-rate fabulist, phenomenologist, defender of defeated causes, and most usefully here, Eliza's authority on rotten luck. He spoke in slogans that he had read in books. He said: *To each according to his needs, from each according to his abilities.* He lamented: *Time is the fire in which we burn.* He pronounced: *Every man his own football!* He railed: *I think of Germany at night; the thought keeps me awake till light.* Once as he and Eliza rushed through a station to catch a departing train—he made it to the platform first—and he called out to her: *Run, comrade run; the world is behind you.*

And she ran. She grabbed his hand.

She regretted nothing more, nor remembered anything better.

LESSON 14

I would love to see you, but you live so far away now
Ich würde Dich gern sehen, aber Du wohnst jetzt so weit weg

———

Benjamin Leopold, upon opening the letter from his cousin Eliza and reading it aloud to his younger sister, Lemon, tossed the single handwritten page down by the side of the swimming pool. Nearly threw it into the blue water—

Lemon quickly reached and grabbed it up.

Lemon smoothed out the crumpled paper.

She said, "Tell me about the case of Elsa Z."

Ben said, "It's a mystery."

A mystery?

It was their great-grandfather's famous lost case.

Ben said that no one had ever found the actual manuscript written in Dr. Apfel's hand. No one knew what went on between the doctor and his patient in that locked room—his office—in the winter of 1919.

Perhaps there never was a girl called Elsa.

"The story, this story—whatever it is that this woman is promising to tell Eliza," said Ben. "It isn't true. It can't be."

"So?" said Lemon.

The *truth* of it did not matter too much to Lemon. The *truth* was not what was so particularly or peculiarly interesting about it to her.

"Truth," she said, "is an artificial construct."

"Where did you hear that?" he said.

"I didn't *hear* it; I *read* it in *Vogue,*" she said.

He said, "Lou—"

She said, "Don't *Lou* me. I did *so* read it. It was an article about faux fur."

"So there is a woman in Germany who claims to be our long-lost great-aunt, and she writes to our cousin and says that she has a story that suddenly she needs to tell?" said Ben.

Said Lemon, "Isn't it fabulous?"

"Why should we believe her?" asked Ben.

"Why shouldn't we believe her?" said Lemon.

Lemon said that travel is easy these days.

Lemon said that she was going to Berlin.

He said, "Go."

She said, "I will."

He said, "Go already."

She said, "I am."

Lemon, long-legged in her bikini, stood.

She stretched her arms over her head.

"Poor Eliza," said Lemon.

"And what do you think that you can do for her?" said Ben.

"Poor Eliza," Lemon went on, "she has rotten luck."

"And you want to go to Berlin," he said.

"And I *do* want to go to Berlin," she said.

"Because you are bored?" he said.

"To see, to hear the story for myself," she said.

Lemon paused.

She said, "And maybe it will make a good movie."

Said her brother, "So much for responsibility."

Lemon said, "Doctor, Doctor, I feel like a spoon—"

Ben said, "Well then, sit still and don't stir."

Lemon plucked at the strap of her black bikini top from her white shoulder and tilted her head, checking to make sure that she was without trace of either tan or burn.

Lemon's sunblock was scented of lavender.

She said, "Tell me about Hedy. About what *really* happened. Tell me about the accident."

Ben said, "It wasn't an accident. She killed herself."

"Of course *you* say that," said Lemon. "You don't believe in *accidents.*"

"And you don't believe in *truth,*" he said.

"I didn't say that I didn't believe in it," she said, "just that it's artificial."

"Tell me the difference between fake and artificial?" he said.

"So there is no such thing as an *accident?*" she asked. "Nothing is *accidental?* No *chance?* No *happenstance?* No *wrong place at the wrong time?*"

"You tell me," he said.

"What else do you think runs in the family?" Lemon asked.

Ben was an authority on their great-grandfather.

Lemon said, "Doctor, Doctor, I think I'm a deck of cards."

Ben said wearily, "I'll deal with you later."

Lemon asked, "How many psychiatrists does it take to change a lightbulb?"

Ben had read Dr. Apfel's cases and papers. He had studied. And sifted. He had been compelled. He was compulsive. He might even have described himself as *obsessed.* And he worried that he had chosen his profession and field—medicine; psychiatry—out of an obligation to the past, rather than any real conviction on his own part.

Providing, of course, that there is such a thing as *real conviction.* Or *obligation.* Or *belief.* Or *truth.* Or *accident.* Or *choice.* Or *responsibility.* Or *realism.*

Or that the lightbulb really wants to be changed.

Lemon said, "What do I pack for November in Berlin?"

43

Said Ben, "Anna Apfel died in Sachsenhausen."

"But do you know it for sure?" asked Lemon.

He could not say that he knew it *for sure.*

Lemon asked, what in the end, had happened to Elsa Z.?

Ben didn't have an answer to her question.

He said that she was missing *the point*—

He said no one knew *if* there really had been a girl called Elsa, let alone what had happened to her. And just because one wanted—or even needed—to believe that a story was true; well, that certainly didn't make it true.

"Poor dear you—" said Lemon.

She heaved a wonderful sigh.

"So you won't come with me?" she said.

"Well then, what do you want?" she asked. "I mean, what should I bring back for you? A beer stein? A Volkswagen? Oh, what about one of those chocolate oranges? Or a T-shirt—*My sister went to Berlin and all she got me was this lousy*—"

"Proof," he said.

"*Proof?*" she said.

"Of what?" she said.

Ben did not answer.

He drank.

He paused.

He pondered.

"Proof—" he repeated.

"Oh," said Lemon. "A Volkswagen might be easier."

Ben closed his eyes.

She considered.

She said, "All right—*proof.*"

"Be careful," he said.

Lemon looked at her brother.

"It's Germany," she said. "What's the worst that could happen?"

LESSON 15

All sailors are on deck
Alle Matrosen sind an Deck

———

How do you pass the time on trains and buses, in automobiles, and on airplanes? In the darkness, do you close your eyes? Are you fond of working crossword puzzles, playing cards, writing letters, turning a magazine's pages, dozing, dreaming, or gazing out the window? Have you brought along a book? And if so: what have you chosen to read? Do you favor romance? Or follow the exploits of vampires? Are wizards worth your while? Do you study biographies of movie stars? Or take solace in the solemnity of scientific tomes? What about foreign language dictionaries, in which each new word is rife with meaning? Or glossy guides containing maps to scenic sites: to castles, churches, concentration camps, and battlefields? Do you like inspirational stories of hope, healing, and redemption? Or does the dark side of human nature have an intoxicating appeal?

Germany is the land of fairy tales, forests, magic mountains, and the Brothers Grimm.

Gutenberg invented moveable type.

Goethe demanded: *More light!*

Faust signed with the devil on the dotted line.

Martin Luther nailed his 95 Theses upon a church door in Wittenberg; and the sound of his banging hammer echoed in Rome.

Heidi Klum graced the 1998 cover of the *Sports Illustrated* swimsuit issue.

Claudia Schiffer's autobiography, *Memories,* tells of her happy barefoot Bavarian childhood; describes her discovery by the director of a top modeling agency; and documents her rise to her unassailable position as Karl Lagerfeld's muse. Photos throughout.

All things are possible.

As Hansel and Gretel to the forest; so your fears to the oven.

In Germany: mysteries, political thrillers, true crime novels, and accounts of brave men who have survived disasters at sea are very popular.

LESSON 16

How much does it cost?
Wieviel kostet das?

―――

At a shop in the airport, Lemon purchased a travel dictionary.

And a copy of *Tangled Ravages* by Justine St. Ives.

As she waited in the terminal, she began reading the novel. At first she thought it was silly; the jacket promised: a story of star-crossed lovers! Julia Fitch Devereux, the young beautiful unhappy wife of Dr. Fielding Devereux, a wealthy old distinguished disinterested surgeon, was falling for Wilder Penn, a handsome tortured scientist with a mysterious past. Where was he from? Where had he been? Wilder's duty to science precluded his desire for Julia—so far—no wait—Lemon flipped ahead—in the library of Julia's exquisite country manor, there among the beau-pots, lilies, and leather-bound tomes; under the watchful eyes of marble statues; upon the velveteen sofa they succumbed to forbidden passion! Off off off trembling shoulders slipped Julia's white gown. How her bare skin—*like alabaster—porcelain, silk, oh!—nacreous nethers*—glowed in the candlelight. And he said, Wilder was saying—

Before Lemon knew it, the first-class boarding of her flight was announced.

LESSON 17

The cat crept carefully closer
Die Katze schlich sich vorsichtig an

———

Because Lemon had so far been lucky, this did not mean that at any moment her luck would not change. There was always a new style with which to contend: a trend to set, a fashion to forge or follow, a public predilection to survive. *It* was hair: blonde or brunette, straight or curly; skin: pale, powdered, tan, glitter-specked, or freckled. It was high heels, hugged hips, and low necklines; it was bigger breasts, smaller ears, toothier teeth; more muscle; less politics; fewer words; more tattoos. It was newsboy hats, horn-rimmed glasses, or tiny dogs toted in purses. It was smart or dumb. One season: irony was in vogue; the next, sincerity became the new irony. And then authenticity replaced sincerity. As opacity waned, transparency waxed. Plastic, leather, cashmere, sackcloth, silk? Who knew which way the edge would cut? Lemon was lucky. Louisa was Lemon. And Lemon was *now;* she was glamorous. She was *then.* She harkened to Hollywood's golden past; she made you imagine the possibilities the future held.

She had seen herself naked projected upon the big screen.

Her flaws were flawless.

Audiences showed fidelity; audiences loved her.

In her last film, *Doctor, Doctor,* she played a psychic.

In the one before that, she was a stripper.

Was Lemon a good actress?

In a recent disaster film she had played a scientist upon whose technical theories and theoretical genius the fate of the world rested during an outbreak of a deadly chimpanzee-borne virus. She was believable. And just because she was not nor had ever been in *real life* a scientist or prescient—or a stripper—did that mean that she couldn't *empathize* or *imagine*? It was not experience that made a good actor, but *credibility;* and credibility was a function of heart. And Lemon had it. Or it had her. The ideal she presented served to make the real seem more so. The unreal proved the possibility of impossibility. And this, Lemon Leopold could provide.

She was in search of the perfect role.

Something that suited her strengths and made her weaknesses irrelevant. Something that suited her weaknesses and made them into strengths.

How—and where—did one find a story like that?

Lemon checked in at the best hotel in the Berlin under the alias Plum Peabody. She inquired only half-jokingly about the thread-count of the sheets.

LESSON 18

You will not escape punishment
Ihre Strafe wird nicht ausbleiben

———

Let the critics criticize and the dreamers dream. Eliza wrote romance
novels. She turned out potboilers under the *nom de plume:* Justine St.
Ives. Her books weren't of literary merit—too obvious, atrociously
cloying, impossibly predictable—but were embraced by a legion of
loyal readers who crave dependability in a paperback. Her narrative
knack was limited to melodrama. Her abilities were modest. And her
few tricks—rabbits out of hats; deceit and décolletage; arrow-pierced
apples; trains into tunnels; symbolism and surrender—timeworn. She
did not analyze desire or ramble waxy with philosophical abstractions.
She provided scenery, situation, and seduction—the Seine *avec* Pierre
by moonlight; Venice via a rugged-shouldered gondolier; the
coxswain-muddled treacle of the Thames—only tortured men and
beautiful women of tragic circumstance. And in each story, she was
not ashamed to admit, the hero was based in no small part, and not
unconsciously, on Hart Luther. The strangest thing of all? He sold.
The more the hero resembled him in spirit, in character, pound for
word-weightless pound, noun for adjective, in woe and wild-eyed happiness alike, the faster the book flew from the shelves. She dressed him
up in various guises: soldier, sailor, aviator, prince, journalist, and jail-
bird. But underneath the costume you would always find Hart the
fanatic, the genius, the crazy Jew, the dead man.

When Eliza met Hart, she was eighteen; she described herself in a line lifted from one of her favorite books: *at eighteen I was conspicuously retarded*. He favored—and who can blame him?—a more fiery sort of girl: showstoppers; activists; protestors who threw their bodies in front of bulldozers, lashed themselves to ancient redwoods, shouted, harassed, marched, picketed, and painted placards promoting their hatred of hate. He fell for sturdy tattooed beauties in combat boots; graduate students in massage therapy; fans of Foucault; lovelorn leftists; strippers; teen mothers; and nonstop argument igniters. Eliza was shy and shadow-bound, but she had something the value of which she was not aware—a hold on the past—a heredity that could not be denied. And Hart grew mad for it.

Hart found in Eliza the most willing of listeners. Insomniacs both, at night they played a game of their own invention, and they called it Traveler.

The traveler travels, they said, from place to place, from story to story, and you never knew where he would appear and in what disguise.

The game always began with a question: *what happened next?*

It never occurred to either of them not to answer.

Hart wanted to smash all that was wrong, unfair, unjust, and unjustifiable. Being quiet was a colossal waste of time. Lamentation was for chumps. Where would wallowing get you? Nowhere! Rumination was the cancer of the intellect. As modern—no—as *postmodern*—as he was—you could smell the dust of history on his skin. For all of his change-evincing, future-dreaming, tub-thumping, torpedo-damning ideology, Hart Luther lived in the past. Nothing was more immediate to him than the faraway. The Crusades? The destruction of the Temple? The Babylonian captivity? He felt the fall of whip and lash; he, himself, and no stand-in, no signatory, no angel. He had blisters from bricking Egypt's great pyramids. Is it possible that he knew too much? That he had lost his mind, his—what's that meaningless word people always use—

perspective? Where iron nails had been run in, his palms and ankles were scarred.

He was regal. He was a riot. He really was.

Hart asked: *Did you know that Kipling accused Einstein of distorting the very fabric of reality to further his "devious Jewish agenda"?* He collected facts. He kept track of atrocities. He was plagued by intricate patterns of probability. Nothing escaped him. Hart was manic. Hart was depressive. Ezra Pound, Henry Ford, and Walt Disney were war criminals. Hart had questions: *What point is the mapped-out maze of history—the crimes, the triumph and torture iterated and itemized—if we don't use it to navigate our future? And how do we escape the paradox of being forever in thrall? First the Nazis murder our families, destroy our past, and then they force us to mull the hideousness of them and their sins for an eternity?*

Hart joked: *Come the revolution we'll eat strawberries and cream.*

He lowered his voice into a dictatorial threat: *And you'd better like it.*

Back then: Eliza may have been innocent, but she was never naïve. She knew that Hart saw her as the great-granddaughter of Dr. Jozef Apfel. It was only a shame that the relevant inheritance was on her mother's side; names were important to Hart. But really, look at it from his point of view. He often spoke of destiny. His family was a ragtag pack of dreamers; hers was in the business of decrypting dreams. How could she continue to write love stories? Hart Luther walking the plank in a pirate getup, with an eye patch and parrot? Hart Luther as a cop on the beat? An idealistic young poet? A lifeguard teased by the tales of mermaids? Every hero and each villain that she put to pen was part and parcel the same character. She was trying to resurrect him, if only for a few moments, trapped in and on the confines of ink and paper. She would not give up the ghost of him.

LESSON 19

The girl is pretty; the hand is clean
Das Mädchen ist hübsch; die Hand ist sauber

―――

What did Eliza remember?

There was a man up in the bell tower with a rifle. He had it balanced on his shoulder. And down below, students had begun to congregate; everyone looking upward. There was no need to shield one's eyes, because it was overcast and cloudy; no sun. Someone from the astronomy department ran to get binoculars. And the police arrived. They talked to the man through a megaphone. They said: *Be reasonable.* And: *Do you have any demands? What are your demands?* The police put up a barrier to keep the students back, but it didn't do any good. Everyone waited. Eliza stood looking up. She was eighteen; she was naïve, if not entirely innocent. She had taken a shortcut back from the library through the courtyard. Now she waited in the January cold looking up at the bell tower for the gunman to: shoot. Or be reasonable. Or make a demand. A girl in a ski jacket with ice skates slung over her shoulder said: *Doesn't this just take the cake!*

A young man standing beside the girl leaned close to her and said something. Just then the students gathered in the cold in the courtyard before the bell tower with the broken bell that never rang heard a shot. It was not the man with the rifle. The shot came from a window in the physics building. A police sniper—or was it a sharpshooter? The man in the bell tower was hit. Everyone saw it happen. There was silence. No one spoke. The man was hit and fell forward. The rifle fell first, and then he tumbled after; a body falling from the tower.

Who realized it first? Who saw clearly against the cloudy gray sky?

The dummy lay dull and unharmed on the ground. There was no need for an ambulance. The police took away the wooden barricades. It was a training exercise. Because of the bomb threats. Someone kept calling in bomb threats on girls' dormitories. The administration suspected several radical student groups. Letters had been sent home to parents. But the threats kept coming, and night after night girls filed out of their dormitories in the darkness. Eliza had gotten in the habit of sitting in her room fully dressed, waiting for the sirens.

When the body came falling from the bell tower to the stunned silence of the students waiting down below; when it became apparent that it was not a person but a dummy, the young man standing beside the girl with the ice skates broke the silence and yelled: *You fucking fascists!* And then other students started to yell. And someone hurled a bottle at a police car. And the girl tugged him away by the arm, but he kept looking backwards over his shoulder at the body, and the broken glass, the toy rifle, at the police trying now to restrain the screaming students. Eliza thought that for a moment he looked right at her, and that their eyes met in some great and sad understanding. She was certain of it. But months later when she asked Hart Luther about this, about that day in the courtyard with the police sharpshooter, he didn't remember her. And he asked with surprise: *Were you there?*

LESSON 20

Shall we go to the sea today?
Wollen wir heute ans Meer fahren?

Lemon Leopold was absolutely starving.

She had had no supper the previous evening after her exhausting journey. From the room service menu she ordered up: coffee in a silver pot, with sugar and cream; *Brötchen,* butter and strawberry jam; hard-boiled eggs, cheese, and cold sliced ham. It was a damp morning—make that very nearly afternoon—and in her pajamas, as she added cream and stirred her coffee, she began reading the next chapter of *Tangled Ravages.*

She found Julia and Wilder just where she had left them.

Here they were awaiting her—

They met for an afternoon tryst in a seedy motel in a dangerous part of town.

While Wilder slept, Julia stood naked at the window.

Lemon sipped her coffee.

Julia wrapped herself in the muslin curtain and looked down at the street below. The thin, threadbare fabric clung to her hot, damp skin. The last of the setting sun caught and illuminated golden her fair hair. Down below in an alley, she saw men rolling dice. She saw police running after a thief. She felt danger all around her! She was on fire! Her body trembled with desire and anticipation. She could not sleep. Julia harbored a secret. She turned her diamond wedding ring round and round on her slim ring finger. How could she tell Wilder her secret? Did she dare demand of him the very thing that he would not ask of her?

The chapter ended.

Lemon used as a bookmark Eliza's letter.

She tucked it between the pages.

She ate with her fingers one last and lonely salted egg.

Then, in no particular hurry, she dressed.

In the lobby of the hotel she signed an autograph for a darling little English girl. The girl, no more than ten years old, had red-ribbon-tied braids and wore a peacoat. Shyly, sweetly, demurely, she asked: *Oh, please, Miss Leopold—?*

Lemon was polite, but she was wary of darling children. She had only recently been one herself.

LESSON 21

What happened?
Was ist passiert?

———

Conspicuously incognito with her fair hair under a wool cap, in a cashmere coat, a short skirt, fishnet stockings, and high boots, Lemon Leopold blazed through Berlin. She knocked on the door of Eliza's hotel room. Knock, knock. How do you exit in case of emergency? Who's there? You don't: *you exist.* Eliza answered the door. "Let's get out of here," Lemon said to her.

LESSON 22

Price is determined by supply and demand
Angebot und Nachfrage regeln den Preis

———————

Lemon and Eliza sat in a café on the Bleibtreustrasse.

Pictures of long-ago film stars lined the walls.

Marlene Dietrich in *The Blue Angel.*

Greta Garbo in *Grand Hotel.*

"Ben has gone dark," Lemon said.

"What's the matter with him?" asked Eliza.

"He's *in crisis,*" said Lemon.

"Will you split a piece of cake with me?" she asked.

"I haven't been hungry since I got here," Eliza said.

"Everything looks so good," said Lemon.

She looked around the crowded café.

She gestured for the waiter.

She pointed to the plate of a man at a nearby table: *that please.*

"Wouldn't it be funny," she said, "if he brings me something completely different? No matter what he brings, I won't send it back. Unless it's the head of a pig with an apple in its mouth, something horrible like that."

"*Schweinefleisch,*" said Eliza.

"You're going dark too," sighed Lemon.

"He'll bring you cake," said Eliza. "He'll bring you the most beautiful cake you've ever seen, because—"

"I'm a movie star?" Lemon said, laughing.

"Because it's his job," said Eliza.

"So tell me the story," said Lemon.

"I can't believe that you're here," said Eliza.

"What was I supposed to do? I got your letter, and I wasn't doing anything. I was—you know?—between things. And I wanted to *do* something. So I hopped a plane. But I couldn't get Ben to come with me. Why don't you move over to my place? It's so much better than yours. And it looks right out over the zoo. You don't have to get a room; you can stay with me; it's fucking palatial. God, I'm absolutely starving," she said. "Why is everyone staring at me?"

"It could be the sunglasses," said Eliza.

"You don't like?"

The cake arrived.

Lemon asked, "You won't tell my mother will you?"

"Why would I tell your mother?" said Eliza.

"Ben is miserable. He's going Oedipal," said Lemon.

"I thought Ben was going dark," said Eliza.

"Dark and Oedipal," said Lemon.

"Try some of this, will you? Don't make me eat it all myself," she said.

Lemon looked at her plate.

"Tell me about the old lady," she said.

"I haven't seen her," admitted Eliza.

"You haven't *seen* her?" said Lemon.

Eliza said, "I tried, you know; I *tried,* but I just couldn't."

"Why not?" asked Lemon.

"I was waiting," said Eliza.

"For what?" said Lemon.

"What for?" said Lemon.

"I don't know," Eliza said.

"A sign, something—A symbol—?" Eliza said.

"Fuck symbols," Lemon said.

"Fuck fate," she said.

Eliza watched the waiter.

He was taking an order.

Upon the wall:

Dr. Caliguri lurked.

Metropolis awaited.

Lemon was happy that Eliza had waited.

Lemon wanted to hear the story from the beginning.

And Eliza knew this.

Eliza turned her spoon in her cup.

Lemon said, "I can do a German accent. Do you want to hear?"

"How's the cake?" asked Eliza.

"Fabulous," said Lemon.

LESSON 23

The fire is continuing to spread
Das Feuer greift weiter um sich

———

Travel is easy these days. Go light. Just pack a small bag. Everything you need will be awaiting you on the other side of your journey. Eliza went to Berlin. And you should too. She took a taxi to the airport. She boarded a plane. In Amsterdam she changed planes and traveled on to her terminal destination. In Berlin she took a taxi from the airport to the hotel. She asked for the room. She specified the room number. Even the key felt familiar. *My name is Eliza Berlin, and there is nothing—no wait, there is something—particularly and unstoppably German about me.* She pulled open the curtains to stare out at the rain-damp November dark city. Her great-grandfather Jozef Apfel was a psychiatrist who had treated a girl called Elsa Z. The doctor had written a famously revered and authoritative treatise on the unconscious underpinnings of humor entitled *Jokework*. Eliza wrote romance novels. For who is lonelier than the romance novelist? And who craves order more than the disorderly? And who is less right than the wronged? Dr. Apfel had two children, Franz and Anna. Franz had three daughters: Amalie, Hedy, and Petra. Amalie had a son named Ben and daughter called Lemon. Ben wanted proof of the past; Lemon really enjoyed solving riddles. Hedy had a daughter called Eliza. Eliza knew a boy named Hart Luther. He died. Most people do. What happened next? One day a letter came to Eliza in the mail from a woman who either was or was not Anna Apfel; and Eliza—packed a bag; left her home; purchased a ticket; boarded an airplane; departed; arrived; to return, returning—returned to the city which bore a name that her father did not so much inherit as borrow; back to the very room—foreign, familiar—where she and Hart spent their last nights together.

Eliza came to Berlin to see it for herself.

She was not in search of sweeter adjectives to blot out bitter nouns.

She was here to hear a ghost story.

LESSON 24

I prefer to eat cake
Ich esse lieber Kuchen

———

Who was Elsa Z.?

Madame Madeline Apfel spent many pleasant afternoons together over sweets and sheet music with a girl whom the doctor would later have occasion to call Elsa Z. During the course of one such lesson, the girl fell violently in a seizure across the keys and down from the piano bench to the floor. Elsa, when roused moments later with the aid of salts from her collapse, cried out; for she could neither feel her arm nor move the fingers of her right hand.

LESSON 25

They didn't let the hostages leave the plane
Sie liessen die Geiseln nicht aus dem Flugzeug

———

Frau Marx shooed away a cat from the table—

Upon which she had set cups and spoons and saucers and a teapot.

There was cream. And there was sugar.

She asked, "Would you like to pour the tea?"

Lemon poured the tea.

Eliza held the cups for her cousin: one, two, three.

Frau Marx (*no, no; call me Anna*)—said that she wouldn't have bothered the girls—not with the past—if she hadn't become overcome as of late—with such strange dreams.

She had learned long ago from Father that one couldn't underestimate the importance of a dream, in the literal and figurative senses alike.

Our obligations begin in dreams.

This story that she was going to tell—

Lemon leaned forward upon the sofa.

And resting her teacup upon her palm, she held the handle with her slim fingers.

Lemon said, "I don't mean to be rude, but really, this is all so strange. I mean, we thought that you were dead."

"And what do you think now?" Anna asked.

Lemon laughed.

In that way that she did.

When she thought that something was funny.

Threw back her head, laughed.

Like a girl in a movie.

Lemon had the slightest bit of a German accent.

Eliza heard—didn't she?—a piano.

Anna had lived for a time in England.

She didn't want to talk about that.

When they could be speaking of the interpretation of dreams.

A dream may have so many meanings.

And after all, one place was not so different from the next.

The gray cat leapt upon the table.

"Try some cake," said Anna.

There was a cake upon the table.

Wasn't that gray cat curious?

Look, isn't the sun breaking through the clouds?

The piano player stumbled.

The music stopped.

Then resumed.

Lemon took the knife.

And cut into the chocolate cake.

Anna removed her eyeglasses.

She rubbed clean the lenses with a white handkerchief.

"I am so happy," said Frau Marx, "that there are three of us."

She didn't like to lament the past.

Though she did question now and then—

When it came around to it—

Could things have been different?

Eliza and Lemon sat upon the sofa; the low tea table before them.

A black cat with white boots slept on the window seat.

The gray cat crept curiously toward the cream.

The cake—do you like it?—came from that bakery around
the corner.

The apartment—in the modern building of shining metal and glass—was bright and comfortable. A Turkish girl came in three days a week to do the cleaning.

Anna held out to Eliza a photograph of two girls in aprons.

"This is Tulla. And that is Dolfi."

Anna dropped a sugar cube into her cup. For years she had given up thinking about the past. It is better to live in the present. Even now—she looked to the future. To the latest novel—

Anna confessed: she had a weakness for detective novels. Don't you agree that there is something very satisfying about the resolution of a mystery?

Could things have been different?

Lemon sipped her tea.

Eliza studied the picture.

Two grinning girls stood caught against the gate in the sunny garden.

Was it distance or distortion that made them seem so spun-sugar sweet and perfectly porcelain tiny—or was it a trick of time?

Anna said, "Mother was beautiful and Father was important."

And so began her story.

LESSON 26

Before going, he kissed her
Bevor er ging, küsste er sie

———≈———

How good was Anna's memory?

She grew up in a grand house on the Kurfürstendamm with her
father and mother and brother. They had a maid and a cook. The
maid was Tulla; the cook, Dolfi. Mother wore black. Mother was
Madeline. Franz was Anna's older brother. He was a dreamer. He
closed his eyes to the world. Father was a scientist. Father studied the
workings of the mind. His patients visited him in his office. When
Father was with a patient, she knew—Anna knew—she must be very
quiet and not run up and down the stairs or slam doors or sing too
loudly or turn the handle on his office door.

She knew the house room by room.

In his office Father sat before his typewriter.

In the kitchen Dolfi salted sausages. And Tulla, looking on, laughed.

In the garden Franz slept under the shade trees.

Plums hung from bough and branch; roses climbed the
unlocked gate.

In the parlor Mother sat at the piano.

In the evening Father's students came around for tea and cream
cakes on flowered plates. Father's students asked questions. They
talked about problems. They spoke of solutions. There were arguments and accusations. Father listened. He sighed. He heard all sides
and then he spoke; he explained who was right and what was wrong.

How good it was to have a father who knew what was right and who was wrong.

How nice to have a mother who wore pearls roped about her neck.

How nice to have a brother with whom to piece together puzzles.

And a dog who would give his paw to shake.

How nice to sit drawing pictures upon the scrolling roll of butcher's paper at the kitchen table between Tulla and Dolfi while they told stories.

When she was four years old, Anna met the girl called Elsa Z.

Anna was walking with Mother in the zoological garden. Anna ran on ahead chasing after her ball; Anna's ball rolled to Elsa, who sat on a bench. Elsa picked up the ball. Elsa was crying. Mother sat with the girl. Anna wanted to see the monkeys. Mother sat with the girl for a long while. Mother and Elsa soon became fast friends, and along with Anna they walked the paths of the zoo.

Elsa had large gray eyes.

She gave to Anna cinnamon candies and little wrapped sweets.

Anna took Father's dog on his leash.

Falki was Father's chow dog.

Mother and Elsa walked arm in arm.

And for a time: Oh! They were not to be separated.

They sat together at the piano.

Then Elsa fell ill.

Elsa had fallen ill. She could not play the piano. She could not sit at the piano bench with Mother, the two of them playing in time together across the black and white keys.

Elsa stopped visiting Mother.

One day Elsa came back to the house.

She came to see Father.

She was to be Father's patient.

For Elsa was ill.

Father was going to cure her.

Father was Dr. Jozef Apfel.

If there were a solution to Elsa's problem, Father would find it out.

And whether one likes it or no, there is always a solution to a problem.

LESSON 27

She follows me like a shadow
Sie folgt mir wie ein Schatten

———

Jozef Apfel married his first wife in 1896.

Her name was Klara. She was eighteen. Young, beautiful—

She had white skin and an ornate knot of blonde braid pinned up with black ribbons.

Her eyes were *Dromboorv* blue.

Like blackberries.

She was not quite right in the head.

Which is only to say: her mind was mysterious.

Her husband adored mystery. Her husband adored her.

Klara was not timid or intractable.

Klara always wore white.

Her father gave them as a wedding gift the grand gloomy house.

She could be found sitting in her garden in all weathers—even in the rain and snow.

Klara gave birth to their only child, Franz, in 1899.

When Franz was born, the family celebrated.

The following year Dr. Apfel, whose face had begun to look older and more venerable, more solemn, by the day, achieved a sudden though not unwanted notoriety for a work he published, *Udo A.: An Analysis of a Case of Psychosexual Crypto-Comedic Dementia.*

The study—the explicitly detailed exploits of a soldier called Udo, who boasted possession of the ability to seduce women by telling jokes—was taken up by readers outside of the medical field for the delightful perversity of the narrative.

The doctor began to develop his triangular seduction theory.

The doctor's reputation grew. And patients followed: ladies in fur and gentlemen with gold-tipped walking sticks arrived at Dr. Apfel's office.

In 1901 Queen Victoria died, and Walt Disney was born.

In 1903 the silent moving picture *The Great Train Robbery* terrified audiences with its ending: a bandit shooting directly into the camera.

Dr. Apfel favored dark formal coats.

Klara wore white—gauzy dresses: white upon white with embroidery and lace. The fabric under the lace was cut away, revealing the fair unfreckled skin of her arms and neck.

She had a Pomeranian dog—named Her Imperial Majesty Queen Isabella of Spain but called with a belly rub and ear scratch, Pflaume—

Franz chased Mother's little dog back and forth from the house to the garden wall.

In 1904, in 1905, in 1906—

J. J. Thomson theorized that electrons were imbedded in atoms like raisins in a cake.

Berlin and Paris were linked by telephone.

Ladies wore picture hats piled with flowers, ribbons, stuffed birds, and feathers.

Dr. Apfel read aloud his papers, *his cases,* to full lecture halls.

He was greeted with applause and jeers. He had critics. And enemies. His work was called *the Jewish Science.* His critics asked: *Why should past experience define future behavior?* His enemies wondered: *Why can't he just live and let Oedipus be?* His nights were late. His conclusions were conclusive. His definitions were definitive. He paced his office. He typed. He smoked. His pen scrawled against paper. He lost track of time. Upstairs, Klara read aloud Italian tales about ghosts to Franz. She turned the pages of English novels that took place in drafty castles. She peeled apples with a pearl-handled pocketknife. She pulled her fair hair back into a braid, knotted it up around itself and tied it with a black ribbon. She sat in the darkness by Franz's bed to protect him from specters who stole the souls of sleeping children.

Klara took ill.

She wept. She spoke to shadows—to people whom no one else could see—

She grew weak and wild-eyed.

Her cheeks took on a feverish pallor.

In 1907 Jozef sent Klara to a sanitarium.

In 1908 fountain pens became popular.

And Klara died, as all good heroines should: young and beautiful—of consumption.

Franz knew, though he did not tell his father, that his mother's ghost visited him at night, sitting again at his bedside. She wore her white dressing gown. She grew younger; she came to him as a girl with her peaked face, her ribbons, her funny little dog, her blackberry-blue eyes and apple-peeling fingers.

He knew that she had been in the garden.

Because she smelled of snow.

He knew when she had been in the kitchen.

Because she kissed him good-night and he could taste chocolate.

In 1911 the *Mona Lisa* was stolen from the Louvre.

In 1912 the British luxury liner *Titanic* struck an iceberg.

In 1913 Dr. Apfel met Mademoiselle Madeline in Paris.

He was delivering a lecture entitled *She Laughed: Biblical Sources for an Interpretation of the Tri-part Humor Paradigm.* Madeline sat in the front row taking notes. She wore a black dress and a hat banded with velvet crepe. He saw her serious face. He was caught up with the way her pencil captured on paper his phrases. Madeline, at twenty-four, was a determined spinster. Within a week, he asked her to marry him; they walked in the Bois. He told her about Berlin. He asked her to come to Berlin. For though one could no longer find the wonders of the ancient world, see the antiquities of Illyria, nor pass through Ishtar's gate to great fallen Babylon, one could yet see Berlin. He made her a reasonable and rational case. He asked again. She pondered his question as they walked. The sun passed behind a cloud. Doesn't it look like rain? She saw a little boy poking a dead bird with a stick. She did not believe in omens. A nanny took the boy by the arm and scolded him. And Madeline said yes to the doctor's proposal.

While in Paris, damp and gray, the doctor was asking Madeline to commit to a dream world; back in Berlin, Franz sat in the garden under the shade of the lime trees, his sketchbook fallen to his side. His eyes were open, but he was neither asleep nor awake. And although on the grand timeline, things were happening, and about to happen, near and far—his father would remarry; the second Balkan War was breaking out; Charlie Chaplin was making movies; the fox-trot was all the rage; and zippers were becoming a new standard in clothing fashion—the afternoon was hot and still and perfect for Franz Apfel in the garden.

Dr. Apfel married Mademoiselle Madeline.

And the second Frau—that is, *Madame* Madeline—Apfel took up residence in her Berlin home. Tulla came on as the housemaid; Dolfi followed as the cook. The doctor's household, which had been quiet and day to day unchanging, plates of potatoes and plates of meat, awakened now with not one young woman, but three. Madame played at the piano in the parlor. Dolfi, in the kitchen, rolled out dough with a floured rolling pin. Tulla drew open the curtains in the doctor's office in the morning; she pulled and fastened the curtains closed at night.

In 1914 Archduke Franz Ferdinand was assassinated, and the Great War began.

Passports were made compulsory for foreign travel.

In 1915 Anna Apfel was born.

A German U-boat sank the British liner *Lusitania;* Albert Einstein published his *General Theory of Relativity,* D. W. Griffith delivered *Birth of a Nation.* Where was Franz Apfel—working his sums, supping on soup, asleep in his bed? Franzchen studied German literature, history, biological sciences, Latin, Greek, English, French, and mathematics at the boys' gymnasium. He took classes in drawing, tumbling, and penmanship. He was sickly, everybody said, everyone agreed. He may not have been right in the head. His eyes had a soft unfocused quality that no spectacles could remedy.

Franz took the world as he found it.

Franz loved Tulla.

He loved how when they played croquet, and she lost, she would chase after him to the far stone wall with the mallet, as though to beat him, but at the last moment, just as she overtook him, she would fall laughing into the grass.

Franz loved Dolfi more.

In 1916 Coca-Cola began using a new contoured bottle.

In 1917 there was revolution in Russia and the abdication of the czar; in America Buffalo Bill Cody died, and girls in Paris, London, and New York were bobbing their hair.

And then the war ended. In 1918 Germany signed the armistice. The Romanovs were murdered. And twenty-two million people died worldwide in the influenza epidemic.

In 1919 Ernest Rutherford split the atom.

And Elsa, don't forget Elsa Z., walked into a doctor's office. She said, *Doctor, Doctor, it only hurts when I breathe.* And the doctor said, *so don't breathe.*

In 1920 Franz Apfel left Berlin.

Franz could toss a coin into the air ten times and announce with perfect accuracy—while his hand palm-down still covered the fall—the order, again and again, of heads or tails. He was lucky like that. He left his home and ran off to Paris to elope with a girl called Charlotte Blau. When Picasso saw Charlotte Blau through the window of a café, he—with a napkin still tucked into his collar and waving a soupspoon—chased after her, hurling compliments and curses. The city was just as Madame Madeline had recounted to him so many winter evenings from memory: the language chimed like bells; the streets twisted like an endless argument; the sweets more sweet, the cream more buttery; the rain more wet; the damp less dismal. In a photo studio in the Jewish Quarter, Franz and Charlotte stood and sat, respectively, for a wedding portrait. Is it true about Picasso? Who can say? The photograph captures them in silvery light: her brown dress, his dream-dazed eyes, his distant expression, her dark foreknowledge. They must have done what other young lovers did: walked the Seine, sipped coffee, ate bread and chocolate, remarked on the rotten news in the papers, stared up at the sky and wondered about the possibility of rain. Although neither politics nor intuition—no, it was love—drove Franz Apfel from his home, his bride had her own reasons for restlessness.

LESSON 28

I saw a good film on TV recently
Neulich habe ich einen guten Film im Fernsehen gesehen

———

What did Elsa dream?

I am going to a funeral. I am wearing a white dress. And I don't want to go inside the chapel, because everyone is wearing black. And I have forgotten to wear black. The women are wearing beautiful black dresses and hats pinned with violets, but my white dress is as shapeless as a pilgrim's sack. And the man at the door tells me that I must go in; he says: This way! Hurry please! *But I don't want to go inside and instead I run.*

LESSON 29

People often think I'm a foreigner
Ich werde oft für eine Ausländerin gehalten

———

Lemon Leopold had been pictured in the tabloids very recently sunbathing topless on a yacht belonging to the son of a famous financier. It was rumored that she had run away with him.

This story was—strictly speaking—not true.

She was not the girl in the photograph.

Even though she knew that she was not the girl in the photograph, she had begun to believe that she was. She remembered the salt and the sun. It seemed so real!

Lemon often found herself lost in a story.

When Lemon had played a scientist, she had learned all about evolution.

In her last film, she had played Plum Peabody, a psychic advice columnist.

To more fully understand the nature of the character, she had secretly ghosted for a stint the syndicated advice column *Dear Doctor*.

Lemon had read letters sent in from lonely girls in small towns, from men who harbored secret longings. From grandmothers and virgins and limb-lost veterans. From bullies and the beaten-down and those poor souls whose lives hung in limbo.

And to them she dispensed advice.

To Buddy in Thunder Bay, who had been abandoned by his cheating wife, the Doctor pronounced: *The journey of a thousand footprints begins with a dirty shoe.*

To Holly in Coeur d'Alene, she bolstered: *Do not be downhearted! While it seems impossible that you will ever find true love, remember: certain impossibilities are not that improbable, like winning the lottery or surviving a train wreck.*

To Amber in Embarrass, Minnesota, who was plagued with self-doubt, she commanded: *Eat a peach. Climb every mountain. Be brave and fantastic.*

Tammy in Devil's Lake was tempted.

Kent caught an infection in Spooner.

Harold in Defiance lost his nerve.

In Paradise, Angie dreamed of better.

Buster wanted to play baseball.

Lemon was looking to the future.

There was such a thing as evolution.

All one needed was the will to change.

The desire to be different.

One could learn.

Couldn't one?

To Anton in Providence, she wrote: *Don't be a perpetrator.*

To Emma in Memphis: *Don't be a victim.*

To Raylene in Baraboo: *Don't be a bystander.*

Lemon Leopold had only just come to Berlin and yet she already felt that she knew, she really *knew*—in some deep-rooted way—the girl called Elsa Z.

What is more American than baseball?

What is more romantic than the German soul?

Than the mysteries hidden in a thick dark forest?

Or the bittersweet layers of a chocolate cake?

LESSON 30

Please fasten your seat belt
Bitte machen Sie Ihren Sicherheitsgurt fest

———————

Lemon Leopold stood naked before the gilt-framed mirror in her hotel room.

She was eating a chocolate bar.

"I'm reading *Tangled Ravages*," Lemon said.

Eliza, on the bed, flipped through the television channels with the remote control.

"It's really awful," said Lemon.

"But don't tell me how it ends," she said.

Said Eliza, "Why don't you stop reading it?"

Said Lemon, "I said that it was awful. I didn't say that I didn't like it."

Eliza said, "Not all books are for all people."

Lemon said, "Don't get deep. It's just a love story."

Eliza said, "I'm done with love stories. I mean, who needs them?"

"Needs? Who cares what anyone *needs?*" said Lemon. "Tell them what they *need* and then they'll *need* it. Tell them what to *want* and they'll *want* it."

"You're a fascist," said Eliza.

"I'm so happy," said Lemon.

Lemon leaned her face up close to the mirror.

Lemon had gone to a salon and had her hair colored.

"It's called violet-black," she said. "I had to do it. When I heard the name. It's the name of the character in the movie—that part that Ben *assures* me that I can't get. That's her name, Violet Black. Isn't that funny? Do you think it's funny?"

"What's it about?" asked Eliza.

"The movie? It's called *Alphabet.*"

Lemon touched a hand to her hair.

"Something about a serial killer," she said.

Lemon was just out of the shower.

Eliza said, "I read somewhere that each joke is a tiny revolution."

Lemon saluted herself in the mirror.

"Well, look at me," she said. "I'm a revolutionary."

"Look," said Eliza, "you're on TV. That's you. Isn't it?"

"I'm syndicated," Lemon said. "I'm international."

Lemon put on her silk bathrobe, tied the sash, and sat on the bed.

"It's the one where I find the puppy and hide it in my bedroom," said Lemon.

The dialogue was dubbed into German.

Hund, Hund, cried Sammy Sellars, in a voice that did not belong to Lemon Leopold, as she kissed the golden retriever.

"You know that I didn't really get fired from the show because I grew," Lemon said. "Did you know that?" she asked.

"Really?" said Eliza.

"I slept with my TV dad," Lemon said.

"*Mr. Sellars?*" said Eliza.

Lemon shrugged. "It all worked out for the best."

"Why didn't they fire him?" said Eliza. "Why didn't they arrest him?"

"Have a chocolate bar," said Lemon.

"They cost like forty euros each, no joke," she said.

"No, really, why?" said Eliza.

"I'm so fucking happy," said Lemon.

"Don't be so dramatic," said Eliza.

Said Lemon, "I feel like I'm just getting to know you, to really *know* you."

They watched the television.

"That's what I would sound like if I spoke German," said Lemon.

Her cell phone rang. She answered. While Lemon spoke, Eliza went to the window. She looked out at the city. You really could see the zoo.

There was a travel dictionary on the table.

"You won't believe this," said Lemon. "I got the part."

"I absolutely believe it," said Eliza.

LESSON 31

He really enjoys solving riddles
Rätsel raten macht ihm viel Spass

———

What is the problem with time?

Do conform to the customs and decorum in Berlin. Don't demand. Don't linger. Don't litter. Don't be loud. Don't lament. Don't count. Don't be clever. Don't get cute. Don't curse. Don't cross against the light. Keep off the grass. Don't be callow. Don't complain. Keep on schedule. Don't wish. Don't wait. Don't wonder. Don't wander. Avoid dark streets and dim recollections. Do not expect answers. Don't get theoretical. Don't get deep. Or dramatic. Don't go too ecstatic about the mysteries of life. Be reasonable. Remember: the clock's hands are an invention like anything else. Like the dishwasher, railway car, the printing press, or potato chip. Like the boot, the noose, and the spoon. Invented out of necessity, perhaps; or imagination. What a feat: what we do not know, we want to learn. What we are taught, we turn against. History is what has already happened. What we know, we forget.

What we forget is forgotten.

Don't be embarrassed to ask for directions.

Be polite; in the interest of courtesy, do not ask certain questions.

Don't ask if things could have been different.

Whom can such a question help?

Avoid the obvious.

Obviate accusation.

Ask for symbolism.

Stand on ceremony.

Ask for tales of sedition, seduction, and suicide.

Ask: will I hear tell of wedding cakes and Ouija boards; babies abandoned on doorsteps; brides in white dresses; escape and exile; invention, occupation, and assimilation; West and East; timepieces, taffy, tautology, lice, lemons, lapse, collapse, and confusion; sugar cubes and *crêpe de Chine;* of worsted wool and wanderings; don't forget: genocide, jetsam, and jeremiad; of stockings and syphilis; marzipan, monotheism, bicycles, and back-alley abortions; oubliettes, apostasy, and obligation; wrath, wraiths, and relief; and what about pomegranates and pawnshops; days of drought, rising dough, the dreams of pharaohs, and deepening water?

LESSON 32

Take the medicine three times a day
Nehmen Sie die Medizin dreimal täglich

———

Amalie and her new husband, Mitch Leopold, drove to Niagara Falls. It was supposed to be lovely—Canada—all that clean air and blue water. Amy had a new swimsuit. Mitch had bathing trunks. Finally, they could make use of the heat. How nice to sit by the side of a hotel pool in the sun. It was the honeymoon capital of the world. She wanted to wear her new swimsuit and get a tan. And he would admire her, stretched out and browning, from his chair by the pool. Maybe they would talk about how funny it was that she had said *no* the first time, and *no* the second time, but the third time she came around to the idea of marrying him and said *okay*.

It rained for seven days and seven nights. And it was cold. On the second day of their married life together Mitch and Amy huddled under an umbrella and looked at the Falls in the rain. Then they went to a wax museum and saw figures from horror movies. Frankenstein, Dracula, and the Wolfman were there big as life. Amy bought a postcard from the gift shop. She was going to send it to Hedy and Petra, who loved creature features. She dated the card in her neat handwriting: *June 1961*. But even though she put the card in her handbag, it got soaked, and she threw it out later at the hotel. She caught a cold and by the end of the week, she was glad to say good-bye to Niagara Falls.

Monsters, stories of men going over the Falls in pickle barrels, gloomy afternoons, matinee movies, popcorn and vanilla Coke, the rumpled anonymity of hotel room beds? Hedy would have been mad for it. But Amy wanted to do things the way *normal* people did things. Not crazy people. She wanted to go to Niagara Falls and send home happy postcards that announced: *Here I am in Niagara Falls just like hundreds of other June brides!* She wanted a suntan. She wanted to come home with a suntan and discuss Niagara Falls with recently married girlfriends who had also been there. She did not want to spend a week cooped up in a hotel room waiting for the rain to stop. She wanted to play tennis and meet other honeymooning couples. She did not want to have children right away. She wanted to be a pretty young wife first. And then later, a pretty young mother. She did not care too much for what it was that honeymooning couples did in hotel rooms in Niagara Falls when it was rainy and too cold to sit by the pool.

She sent Mitch out for cough syrup, magazines, and aspirin. He played cards in the hotel bar with other new husbands cast out of their bride's beds in the dreary weather. Amy was twenty years old. Mitch had his own veterinary practice. He had chestnut wavy hair and broad shoulders; he had an older sister; he had nieces and nephews; he had a mother and father, Dot and Jack. Why had Amy said *no* twice before once saying *okay?* Mitch Leopold cared for dogs and cats and even an errant parrot or two. He was in the business of saving lives. Amy should have been the happiest girl in the world. Was she? Mitch told his young wife his secrets on one those of hotel-bound afternoons with nothing but rain and confessions to keep them busy.

To what did Amy confess?

She wore snow-white at her wedding and stood by it.

Amy said *no* twice and then *okay.*

Amy did not confess *everything* to her new husband.

She did not tell him too much about the *truth* of her family.

85

Amy did not tell Mitch about her father, who had relinquished his future to live in a cake-concocting here-and-now rush of the past. About the ghosts who haunted him. She did not tell Mitch about her mother, who lived devoted to her husband's obsessions. She did not talk about her sister Hedy, who was romantic; or Petra, whose eyes had her father's soft unfocused gaze.

Mother and Father wanted their girls to be as American as Coca-Cola.

Father was Franz and Mother was Margot.

When Father was twenty, he left his home: Berlin for Paris. Paris for New York. New York for Detroit. Father was a baker. He baked cakes—beautiful constructions of egg, butter, and sugar—very much in demand, Amy knew, by discerning and fashionable customers.

Mother was an expert in alteration. She could copy any style—any dress out of a magazine. She cut her own patterns. She kept her sewing machine in the kitchen. She sewed Amy's wedding dress, while Father worked at the cake.

Father brought home stray cats and birds and dogs.

Father's cats caught their paws in tangles of thread.

Father met Mother in Paris. Margot was from where? Near Strasbourg. Her father died in the Great War; her mother fell to influenza. What was Margot to do? In Paris she worked as a companion nurse and spent her time in sickrooms consoling fevered ladies. She spooned medicine and heard terrible deathbed confessions. Margot read novels aloud to her patients. She sewed placing one stitch perfectly before the next. Margot learned English placing one word after the previous. When Margot was tall and fair and not too far from childhood, she and Franz came—or went—depending on your direction—to America. And in America they set about baking cakes and sewing dresses and becoming American and having the most beautiful daughters that anyone outside of a fairy tale set deep in the dark Black Forest had ever seen.

The Apfels were dreamers. Amy knew that this was no world for dreamers.

Amy was the only sensible one in the family.

She understood obligation.

Did Amy love Mitch?

Jack and Dot threw Mitch and Amy a welcome-home-from-the-honeymoon party!

Mitch's apple-shaped sister and her potato-shaped husband and their egg-shaped children came to the party, but the Apfels did not: neither Franz nor Margot; neither Hedy nor Petra.

The Apfels were not invited.

Amy envied the normalcy of her husband's family. She admired the Leopolds with their dry store-bought cakes and unsurprising surprise parties. She respected even their spite and cruelty; they were not dreamers. They knew how to get along in the world. Amy envied the Leopold clan, yes, but she knew that she was not, nor would ever really be, one of them.

She did not want them to have possession of certain parts of her.

Amalie Apfel, tall and pretty, with high cheekbones and creamy complexion, blonde of hair and blue of eye, did not too much ponder the past. Why Mitch? Well, he was better than most and as good as some. In Amalie's opinion, he was not *too* Jewish. He stood, like herself, tall and long-limbed. His laugh was authoritative; loud, but not *too* loud. He was not *too* dark or *too* funny or *too* philosophical. He was not prone to bargaining. His father did not see ghosts. Mitch enjoyed a ham sandwich on rye every once in a while without finding his soul was any the worse or imperiled for it, and he believed, as did Amy, in the beneficial effects of fresh air and outdoor exercise on the spirit. Yes, Mitchell Leopold was an excellent example of a modern Jewish husband. At the time, this mattered a great deal to her.

LESSON 33

I am lost
Ich habe mich verirrt

⸻

Ben Leopold sat drinking vodka by the pool in the twilight.

He was slipping: metaphorically. He lifted his glass. He picked up and paged through one of Lemon's scripts from the heap beside him. He was falling: symbolically. He was losing: incrementally. Only a month ago he broke off his wedding engagement, left his practice, and drove across the country from Michigan to California to see his sister, who really, considering the fact that she was twelve years his junior, he barely even knew. His fiancée (now former) was named Elizabeth Albans, but everyone called her Betts. Betts was a blue-eyed blonde with a retroussé nose, the terribly snubby cuteness of which she lamented to her girlfriends. She was in the varied opinions of those who knew her: *beautiful, pretty,* and *cute.* Well, which was it? Ben did not know. Descriptive subtleties were lost on him.

And besides, the distinction between *pretty* and *cute* had nothing whatsoever to do with morality or the meaning of the universe or even actions committed by Betts herself. The difference between *sweet* and *salty* had nothing to do with the way that Betts played tennis or skied or rode horses. At prep school she had been on the field hockey team; she still sometimes liked to wear her little plaid skirt. Betts was *fun* and *flirtatious.* In college she had majored in business. Betts was *brief* and *blasé.* Betts could *bottom-line it.* After Ben asked

88

Betts to marry him, they took a trip to Italy. In Rome—she had been disappointed when men in the street did not try to grab her; she blamed it cheerfully on Ben and on her large diamond engagement ring. Betts was *discriminating* and *discerning*. She was good at nearly everything, and the things at which she did not excel quickly became unimportant to her. After she played tennis at the club, she threw herself into a patio chair and drank gin and tonic with her girl-friends: Kits, Kens, Jes, Jens, Fee, and Josie. Amanda was called Man. Katherine answered to Kat. Kirsten was Kits. Katharine was Kins. And Elizabeth was Ben's invaluable Betts, if only for a while.

Ben stared up at the hazy starless sky.

He had left behind not only his former fiancée, but more impor-tantly, to his point of view, his psychotherapist. And just when they had been making such progress. Just when Ben was on the verge of some miraculous breakthrough. At his last visit Ben had described a sensation that he called *moral seasickness*. And Dr. de Groot asked him if he had been reading his great-grandfather's work again?

What is my problem? Ben asked his doctor.

Betts terrified Ben.

Betts and her bright brilliant girlfriends.

He was in awe of their history. Even if he had to imagine it—

Their great-grandfathers had owned slaves, massacred Indians, felled trees, and manifested destiny. Betts had a Jewish friend named Stephanie who was called Step. Betts called her, *My Jewish Step friend*. And the other girls laughed.

Betts was *clever* and *quick*. Ben was sick at sea.

These mythic great-grandfathers had built houses and surrounded the houses with iron fences, wrought and erected, for the sake of keep-ing generation after generation the likes of Benjamin Leopold away from their daughters. Or at least it seemed that way to Ben.

They were smart superior girls. They had slim hips. They sub-sisted on diet cola, steak, and laxatives. They were *trim* and *toned*.

And if they did not give too much thought to history, let alone responsibility, perhaps it was for the best. Why should Jinx lament upon the past? Why should sadness droop Josie's pert breasts? What had history to do with Kits and Cait? Or Phoebe, called Fee, who was a Daughter of the American Revolution and dressed as a Southern Belle in Fourth of July parades? Or Jens, the pharmaceutical sales representative who stashed samples in her handbag and doled them out to the other girls like candy. Wasn't the allure of Betts her unfurrowed brow? Her unburdened shoulders? That vaguely antiseptic taste of pine on her lips? The bright panzer blue of her forward-looking eyes?

She had already registered for wedding gifts; she wanted to have their towels and linens monogrammed: *Ben & Betts.*

It was *adorable* and *alliterative.*

Betts and her friends went out *en masse* on Saturday nights. They did ecstasy or coke. They didn't like Ben to go out with them. When they were high and happy, he brought them down.

One went to doctors like Lampert de Groot, one sat on the marbled leather sofa in his impressive office to find out about oneself, to come to an understanding of how the mind plays tricks of hiding and seeking; how the body turns against itself. Ben Leopold, in particular, came to Dr. de Groot as part of his own training to become a psychoanalyst. And he continued on visiting Dr. de Groot twice a week. Dr. de Groot, author of the notable treatise on the analyst–analysand relationship called *The Doubletalking Mirror* had a dry sense of humor. *Tell me about your mother?* he joked.

The joke was lost on Ben.

He was like the hapless detective who trampled the crime scene in search of clues only to find that he was following his own bloody footprints. Ben did not want to talk about his mother. His mother had taken Lemon to California when the twelve-year-old landed the part on that television show. His father had stayed behind with his veterinary practice; Mitchell Leopold died of a heart attack alone in

90

that big empty house while his wife and daughter were in Hollywood. Ben was in medical school at the time. Ben knew that it was wrong to blame his mother, but he blamed her nonetheless.

Ben was *myopic*. Lemon was a *movie star*. Lemon did not look too much like her brother. At least that's what Betts said.

Ben broke up with Betts over the phone. *Keep the ring,* he told Betts. She hung up on him. Betts was *fed-up* and *floored*. Betts was *so over it* and *ready to get on with life*.

Ben had a black-and-white photograph of his mother painting his nursery. Father was not in the picture. Father must have taken the picture. Mother gave the camera her starlet's stare. What proof was there of the past? Only, he supposed, that it was gone. That was not enough proof for him. He wanted more. There: in the otherwise empty room stood a cradle pushed off into a corner. It awaited Ben.

It awaited a Ben who had yet to exist.

In the world of the photograph, he would never come into existence.

Ben had gotten *dark* and gone *Oedipal*.

Ben's therapy was not the reason he had left town. Betts was not the reason that he had run. The doubletalking mirror was not the reason that he went to Hollywood. Lemon was not the reason. Mother was not the reason. The photograph was not the reason. What was the reason? Ben was not displeased with the progress of his therapy. He was excavating the unconscious and finding layers of fossils, bones, and ruined antiquities buried just where they should be. But there was something about which he did not tell Dr. Lampert de Groot, who had himself gone through the rites and rituals of psychoanalysis in his youth with the likewise esteemed though now deceased Dr. Morgenstern-Klein of the Vienna school; that he Benjamin Leopold, in the days when he had still been called Benjy, had seen a ghost.

91

LESSON 34

The moon shines into my bedroom
Der Mond scheint in mein Schlafzimmer

———

Eliza hated writing love stories.

Was Hart really a fanatic?

Each joke is a tiny revolution.

The problem with revolution is that it always comes full circle.

Hart was six-foot-four. *Too tall,* he used to say, *too much Jew. Who needs so much Jew?*

Eliza saw Hart in the courtyard that January day when she was eighteen and young and maybe naïve, but not entirely innocent. The girl with the ice skates pulled Hart away by the arm.

Eliza watched them go.

And then she picked up a bottle and hurled it at the police car.

And: nobody owns history.

After that day when the students gathered in the cold to watch the gunman—when she finally saw Hart Luther again months later, she asked him: *If we thought that the man in the bell tower had a rifle, why didn't we run?*

LESSON 35

He wrote to me two years ago, and since then
I've heard nothing more
*Er hat mir vor zwei Jahren geschrieben, seitdem
habe ich nichts mehr von ihm gehört*

———

Lemon and Eliza walked along the Avenue of Limes.

Lemon opened her umbrella.

She held the umbrella over Eliza.

She tried, that is, but Eliza wandered from under the cover—distracted—

They paused before a shop window to admire a pair of black leather boots.

Lemon touched the glass.

Her pale white hand left a smudge on the window.

Eliza said something about cruelty to animals.

Lemon said, "One secret policeman asks another, 'So, comrade, what do you think of the government?' His colleague looks around before answering, 'The same as you, comrade.' Whereupon the first policeman declares, 'In that case, it is my duty to arrest you.'"

Eliza asked Lemon, do you recall?

Do you remember?

Their grandfather Franz had had a dog named Hitler.

Lemon laughed.

Lemon and Eliza made their way in the rain to Anna's apartment.

LESSON 36

Careful, the rope is about to snap!
Vorsicht, das Seil reisst!

———

Anna said that Elsa fell.

And Lemon imagined: Elsa Z. upon the sofa in Dr. Apfel's office.

Lemon Leopold saw the past as a movie.

It was not hard to imagine the long-ago Apfels at home.

The set designers would create a world in chocolate brown.

The costumers would find shoes and hats and dresses!

The house—that shade-shadowed house—

What paradise lay locked behind the wrought-iron garden gate?

Lemon had a problem, and it was this—

She wanted—that is, needed—Eliza, the romance novelist, who to the delight of the lovelorn and consternation of the literary, wrung sweet from bitter, to write the script.

Eliza said that she was through with love stories.

And what was Anna Apfel's story about, if not—in the abstract and the specific—love?

Lemon found the past unfolding before her, act by scene.

As Anna spoke.

And Eliza leaned back against the cushions of the sofa.

And rain pattered the pane.

Lemon was happy.

What good is there in learning about the past, if you choose only to mourn and mope?

It is best not to let the Old World get you down.

What would become of Elsa?

What would happen to the girl who fell paralyzed from the piano bench?

Lemon had learned from her role as psychic Plum Peabody in the thriller *Doctor, Doctor* that belief is the best antidote for disbelief.

Lemon *believed* with a complete *belief.*

Lemon Leopold wanted to play Elsa in the movie.

Because Lemon was an actress, she believed that there existed floating in the pure ether of the universe a movie version of everything and everyone just waiting to be born.

LESSON 37

Anton looks at himself in the mirror and sees
that he is entirely bald
Anton schaut sich im Spiegel an und sieht, dass er ganz kahl ist

———

What about Elsa?

She fell from the piano bench. And her condition worsened in the weeks that followed her fit; her symptoms: digestive difficulties, dizziness, coughing spells, migraine headaches, and morose behavior. Doctors—all manner of medical specialists—examined her and concurred, after finding no somatic explanation or defect responsible for her paralysis, that the girl suffered from hysteria. They prescribed for her regimens of cold hydrotherapy and electrical stimulation, first faradization and then general galvanization; doses of sedative bromides to lower reflex activity, to induce sleep, to subdue excitement of the genital apparatus, and to antagonize congestion of the brain; asafetida—known in folklore as *devil's dung*—to quell hysterical symptoms by driving the wandering womb back into its rightful place; valerian and oil of lavender for nerves; strychnine sulfate for spinal stimulation; and tonic quinine for fevers and exhaustion. When Elsa did not improve—but worsened—with these various treatments, Herr and Frau Z. went to consult Dr. Apfel about a different kind of cure for their ailing child.

The doctor suspected—?

Elsa's predicament to be quite unremarkable. But, for the sake of his wife, the lovely Madeline, who fretted so over the plight of her young friend, whom she had first encountered on a bench at the zoological gardens, he agreed to confer with the girl's parents.

Knock! Knock!

Fine fashionable Frau Frederika and handsome husband Herr Karl Z. arrived at the doctor's house. *Tap, tap, tap*, went his walking stick. *Pat, pitter, patter*, sounded her tiny well-heeled shoes up the steps. And it was with gloved hand that the lady reached up and banged the brass door knocker three hard times. *Knock!*

Tulla swore that—

Frau Frederika Z. gave her the evil eye as she led them down the hallway to the doctor's office. *I felt it burning into my back*, she told Dolfi.

In the office—?

Frederika Z. sat small in stature, diminutive and doll-like, exquisitely attired, with her stockinged legs crossed at the ankles and hands set one upon the other on her lap. Beneath her jacket she wore a loose hip-belted straight-line chemise. Her brown bobbed hair peeked out from under her close-fitting cloche. Though it was a bright and unseasonably warm afternoon, she complained about a draft in the room—*the cold!*—and buried her face up to her pert little chin in the fur that lined her collar. Dr. Apfel shut the windows behind him, but rather than remedy the situation, this further displeased the lady, who announced the room *too close to bear!*

Back in the kitchen—

Tulla bounded in—asked Dolfi who stood stirring with her wooden spoon: *are you making apple tarts?* Wait, wait—before Dolfi could answer, Tulla pulled up a chair at the table, dipped her finger into the bowl, tasted, dipped again, and then did a not very nice imitation of Frau Z.

And in the doctor's office the consultation commenced—?

Frau Z. did not trust maids—shiftless creatures—and she had little regard for hired nurses, nannies, and cooks. Her oldest daughters, Martha and Berit, used to help her with the housework, but now they were both married and had their own houses to keep in order. And Elsa? She was of no use. She fell to daydreaming—and when her mother surveyed the chores the girl had done: there stood pools of suds on the kitchen floor! The lady spent much of her time with Martha and Berit—despite the fact that her two young grandsons so taxed her delicate nerves—and even if it was not her intention, no, no, of course not, her stray comments to each sister about the other drove both girls into jealousy and set them against each other. As she worried and waxed about dust, grime, and dirt; about the city and the country; about her husband's intolerance for rich foods and about the bland dishes that her cook insisted upon preparing; about Theodor, her dear and only son, faraway at the university in Switzerland; as she spoke, Frau Z. adjusted her fox stole, throwing the longer portion over her shoulder with such a sudden violence that she sent rattling a low vase on a nearby table. She turned to her husband and scoffed, *Well there's a fine place to put a table.*

And he said—?

Herr Karl Z. appeared quite healthy, but his wife protested this; no, no, do not be deceived by his appearance! She announced that her husband's physical condition was poor, that she had nursed him back to health from a terrible vigor-depriving illness. The lady worried that her daughter's ailment would prove harmful to her husband's precarious and delicate state.

In the kitchen—
Dolfi asked Tulla, *Does it need it more cinnamon?*

On the stairs little Anna heard—
Maman playing Mozart.

In the office—
Dr. Apfel listened. He deduced, acted on his deductions, relied on his ratiocination to guide him through the inconsistencies—confession is not the problem—everyone confesses—of the case. Herr and Frau told in alternation, one after the other, and each to the next, an obviously fabricated tale of a happy family made unhappy by Elsa's illness. They were at their wits' end. Her mother swore that when cleaning the girl's bedroom she found a suicide note—although when confronted Elsa said it was a poem, and she grabbed the blue paper from her mother, crumpled it up, and stuffed it in her mouth!

What did the doctor deduce?
Though his face showed sincere sympathy and creamy uncurdled kindness, while Frau Z. spoke about her unappreciated and unreciprocated devotion to her children, the doctor awaited the apple tarts that Dolfi was baking.

What was Elsa's problem?
Elsa suffered obsessive and paranoid delusions, which manifested most severely in the fixity of her conviction that she, a girl of nineteen, born with the century, was the target of a grand, murder-minded and plot-driven conspiracy.

What was the doctor's solution?

As the proverb says: *Every madman believes he is the king of France.* The truly difficult part of the psychoanalytic process—the doctor lectured his students—was not diagnosing the problem, but prying—wresting away—pain from the patient. Oh, how a man will cling to the very thing that sickens him most! Why? Because it belongs to him. Because in belonging to him it comes to define him. And a life without the pain of his problem is terrifying, meaningless, and impossible to imagine. Which is to say the neurotic loves his pain more than anything in the world. Because it is his. How locked up tight he keeps it! How he treasures and guards his own prison! How he fears being set free even as he weeps about the torture of his imprisonment! He will tell you that he does not trust doctors. That his problem is special. His problem is without remedy. He believes only in what he feels: pain. One must wrest the keys from the keeper, said the doctor. One must force open the lock!

And how was the doctor to help Elsa?

The girl was haunted by her dreams. And the doctor was known for his interpretive powers. He did not simply *interpret;* he *interpreted his own interpretation.* And herein rested his theoretical skill; for what is more romantic than science?

In the kitchen—

Dolfi placed a tray in the oven.

Down the hallway—

Came Tulla with Madame's afternoon tea.

At the piano bench—

Sat Madeline dressed in black.

In the garden—

Falki, the chow chow, ran in circles chasing butterflies while Franz took from his jacket pocket a folded love letter and read again the words he had long since memorized.

On the stairs Anna overheard—

Someone crying.

Alone in his office—

After meeting with Herr and Frau Z. in his office on a day in October 1919, Dr. Apfel immediately agreed to take up the case.

LESSON 38

Hands up! I have a revolver!
Hände hoch! Ich habe einen Revolver!

———

Ben was reading *Faust*.

LESSON 39

She keeps her jewelry in a safe
Sie bewahrt ihren Schmuck im Tresor auf

⁓

Mrs. Amalie Leopold, wearing a knee-length skirt patterned like a crossword puzzle in black-and-white squares, sat on a bench outside the monkey house at the Detroit Zoo on a day in October 1976. The cold crept up. Winter was on its way. Few people visited the zoo on this raw afternoon, but the concession stand was still open. A girl sold coffee and hot chocolate. She dispensed bags of potato chips and salted peanuts, but not ice cream sandwiches, Nutty Buddy, Drumsticks, Fudgesicles, snow cones, Push-Ups, Good Humor bars, or Bomb Pops; they were gone for the season. Snow monkeys paused in brief patches of sun to pick at each other's fur. And then the sun departed. Mrs. Leopold opened her oversized handbag and took out a fashion magazine. Flipping through the pages, she stopped and attempted to read with some little distraction an article entitled *Heavenly Bodies: Is Cosmic Passion in Your Lucky Stars?*

She wore a black turtleneck sweater under a corduroy blazer. A woolen scarf tied in a loose knot and knotted around her neck was thrown back over her shoulders. Small birds picked and pecked at the remains of popcorn scattered on the ground. The man for whom Mrs. Leopold waited had not yet arrived. She imagined him coming toward her in his khaki and olive drab. The girl working at the concession stand wore a cardigan sweater over a yellow polyester smock. Two young mothers discussed the weather as they pushed their strollers past Mrs. Leopold. *Is it raining?* One asked. The other said, *Not yet, but soon, don't you think?* Her baby slept. The other child was a fat little boy wearing a crocheted blue hat. He stared up at the sky.

Does desire taste like candy? Does it come in a wrapper? Is it like honey or maple syrup? Does it make your fingers sticky? And what if it is not sweet? What if it is salty like the peanuts sold at the concession stand? Maybe it is bitter like medicine, pleasantly unpleasant in its very necessity? When Mrs. Leopold had her wisdom teeth extracted, the dentist fitted a little mask across her face and she breathed deeply until she felt the delirious absence of feeling.

Amy Leopold awaited the man from the monkey house on a day in October.

Is this desire?

The zookeeper was tall but sickly seeming. Nothing about his face made sense. Life in the wild had weathered him. He had not browned to a golden and seamless perfection as had Amalie from summers of lawn-chair naps and suburban indolence. She was exquisite. In a week she would celebrate her thirty-sixth birthday. And though the zookeeper was younger than Mrs. Leopold, he was not so much younger that their meetings were made indecent. No, as she saw it, their trysts were *immoral,* but not *indecent.* He left his sentences unfinished; he answered questions with questions. His black hair already silvered at the temples, like those great fierce mountain gorillas whose pictures she had seen in his books. The monkeys were mad for him. The apes treated him as a comrade. The lesser primates loved him with unabashed abandon. The baboons grew wild at the sound of his approaching limp. The lorises opened their large damp eyes wide with the expectation of his touch. Those tiny elegant creatures called golden lion tamarins allowed him and only him to hold them in the palm of his hand and feed them katydids.

Mrs. Leopold, her legs crossed, looked at pictures in her magazine. The zookeeper didn't take anything seriously. It was thrilling: his all-inclusive, incisive, apathetic pathos. Even his name—Louis Apollinaire—was ironic; or was it romantic? Either way, Louis Apollinaire had *perspective*. He was ahead of his time. But she didn't know, or couldn't yet quite understand, this about him. At this moment, on this particular day in October, she knew only that she was waiting for him and he was late. On this day, he would arrive. One day, he would leave her. Not *her*, of course, not Amalie Leopold in specific, or Amy in general, but the zoo, the city, the cages, the concrete. He would return to his research in the wild.

Little brown birds pecked at popcorn. Amy sat crossword-wise on the bench reading the secrets the stars held for her. Her legs were an unnatural shade of nylon called on the package: *flesh*. A mother walked by holding a little girl by the hand. *Do you want to see the monkeys?* the mother asked. And then Mrs. Leopold heard him. He tapped his way toward her. He did not always use his cane. On those days she recognized the slight *shuffle, drag, shuffle* of his step, not the *tap, tap, tap* that she now heard. Despite his limp, he was not appreciably pitiful. He had the requisite dark humor of an existential evolutionist. The birds scattered, but they would return. The wind blew trash, paper cups familiarly striped red and white: *Enjoy Coca-Cola!* Why did he leave the wild? And where exactly is *the wild* to be found these days? How did he get his curious, though not pity-inducing, limp?

This bicentennial year an unusual number of children readied to dress for Halloween as revolutionary patriots. They would don three-corner hats and capes fashioned out of bedsheets. They would run down the streets yelling: *Trick or treat, smell my feet, give me something good to eat!* And: *The British are coming! The British are coming!* Tiny nightgown-clad versions of Betsy Ross, Florence

Nightingale, and Martha Washington; children disguised as ghouls and mummies, Frankenstein, the Wolfman, and Dracula, Wonder Woman, Spiderman, brides, football players, pumpkins, cats, and cavemen would collect Mars Bars alongside diminutive bewigged Ben Franklins, hobos, the Hulk, devils in red pajamas, and saddle-shoe pompon-waving cheerleaders. *One if by land, two if by sea,* they called out to each other from house to house in the darkness of almost-November.

Was it going to rain? Amy needed to go to the stationery store to pick out invitations for her son's Halloween party. Later, she would do this. Would she select invitations emblazoned with the face of Count Dracula? Or what about funny Frankenstein, green-skinned and monstrously lovable in his undersized sport coat? Benjy was ten. He thought himself too old for the zoo. He preferred lately the dark squalor of pinball arcades. Yet there had been a time not so long ago when he would have forgone anything for a trip to see the seals, the sleeping lions, and tree-grazing giraffes. Do children still love the monkey house? Did they? Maybe people should need invitations to get into the monkey house. It couldn't be very nice to have strangers trampling about day in and out, smudging their fingers against the glass, tapping, making faces, monkey-see, monkey-do. Amalie wanted to remember to ask him about this: why not make the monkey house a little more chic and exclusive, velvet-roped, invitation-only? She knew that he would like the idea. But he would find fault with it. He would frown and say that she was too much of an elitist. How much of an elitist is enough to be? That's what she would ask him if the discussion came around to it; which it would not. She didn't turn at the sound of his footsteps. She looked down at her magazine. At the concession stand, another girl, this one a freckled redhead, joined the girl at the counter in the cardigan sweater. The redhead opened a service window, and both girls leaned on their elbows, window by window, at the counter staring out at the darkening afternoon.

Things retain shadow and memory long past the time of their own usefulness. Soon Amalie Leopold will not be sitting on the wrought iron bench waiting for a man in zookeeper's drab. Just as before she sat there, others occupied that space. Young mothers, impatient fathers, divorcees on first dates, beleaguered babysitters, teenaged truants sipping orange soda, children lost from the group during school field trips, perverts, pedophiles, pensioners, plagiarists, and plainclothes policemen. Piece by piece and bit by bit, the pigeons, the wren and rabbits, the squirrels and sparrow picked away at the popcorn. Nothing would remain. Nothing remained. Mrs. Leopold's magazine would disappear back into her handbag. Cigarette ash on the pavement will vanish. It vanished. It was swept away by broom or wind, washed out by rain. Everything vanished. Everything was displaced. And then replaced. Everything will disseminate. Tomorrow a new magazine will arrive in Mrs. Leopold's mailbox. A new magazine has already arrived in Mrs. Leopold's mailbox. Tomorrow another woman will, would, and did sit and sat on the bench outside the monkey house, anticipating a man who is not and was not and will never be her husband. Today it is Amalie Leopold. She will always have this. The memory of a past forever captured in the present.

The trees branched bare-limbed. Swimming pools long had been emptied. Everything that survived October would become a skeletal version of itself in November. The birds will claw at pebble and stone. The concession stand will close for the season. Mrs. Leopold closed her eyes and listened to the sound of his footsteps, the tap of his cane.

He sat beside her.

"How are the monkeys today?" she asked.

She wore black boots up to the knee. A slight gap of nylon-bright skin appeared between, when she crossed and uncrossed her legs, the hem of her skirt and top of her boots.

"It's raining," she said.

"Words that begin with *R*," he said, "will get you into trouble."

"I don't know what that means," she said. "What does that mean?"

"*M,*" he went on, "is a good solid letter. Nothing to worry about with *M*—"

"I can't stay long."

"But how can you trust a word that begins with *R?*"

"I have to go soon," she said.

The two young mothers passed by again, children in strollers.

"Where is the good doctor today?" he asked.

A blackbird landed beside him on the bench.

The zookeeper moved closer to Mrs. Leopold.

"Lives," he said, "are being saved."

She wouldn't be able to stay long today.

Soon they would not be sitting together on the iron bench.

"Which is better," she asked him, "for a party invitation, Frankenstein or Dracula?"

The concession-stand girls leaned from their windows, watching the zookeeper and Mrs. Leopold.

"Dracula," he said.

"Maybe I should look for ghosts?" she said.

"A vampire," he said, "can't get into the house unless he's—"

"Invited," she said.

"Asked," he said.

They sat in silence.

"That's why you can't send out invitations to the monkey house," she said, "isn't it?"

"How's that?"

"Because of the vampires. You don't want to invite a vampire into the monkey house. Do you?"

"Yes," he said, but he wasn't paying attention. "Are you sure you have to go?"

They did not go to his apartment. They did not move beyond their bench near the concession stand, which had stopped selling ice cream sandwiches, but was still open for popcorn, salted peanuts, coffee, and hot chocolate. On this day she did not have time to go home with him. She had to find invitations for her son's party. She knew that she could purchase a packet of invitations at the drug-store, but she liked the civility of the stationery shop. The Halloween invitations should have gone out days ago, but she had let October slip away, rainy and damp, and now she found herself rushed, and pointlessly so; she had already telephoned the mothers of Benjy's friends. The paper card was only a formality. Today they sat on the bench until it began to drizzle. They discussed nonsense like the saving of lives and the evolutionary ascent of monsters. And she told him that she had to leave.

It was cold. Even for October, it was cold. Children would need to wear winter coats over their Halloween costumes and, despite protests, mittens, while they held out their bags for candy. The little railroad tramps, the lipsticked and rouged-up boy beauty queens, the doctors with stethoscopes and nurses in white tights, the clowns and cowboys, ballerinas, witches, farmers and pharaohs, Oscar the Grouch, Superman, Molly Pitcher, Paul Revere, Daniel Boone, Barbie, Lois Lane, Lewis and Clark, Mason and Dixon, Popeye and Olive Oyl, skeletons and swashbuckling pirates: all would hold out-stretched their bags and pillowcases and plastic pails shaped like pumpkins, anticipating handfuls of sweet and salt.

She left without sentiment. She returned her magazine to her handbag, straightened her scarf about her neck and over her shoul-ders; she walked. She walked away from him in her crossword-puz-zle skirt, her black boots, and corduroy jacket, with her fingers sug-ary from the coffee that had spilled over the side of the cup that she bought at the concession stand before he arrived. He was late. He had been late. Or she had been early. She had crumpled up the cup and tossed it away into the trash before he sat down with her. All things being equal and some not so, time stopped making sense for them, to them. Mrs. Leopold thought of him always in the present. She rose from the bench and left him still seated. He will stand, after she is gone. He will go back to the monkey house, where the monkeys love him—the monkeys, where they are mad for him. He almost forgot his cane. It had slipped to the ground as they sat talking. Small birds, the brown, the black, hopped and hobbled about before flying away. He picked up his cane. He walked, *tap, tap, tap.* Maybe tomorrow or the next day they would find each other again. Words that begin with *R* may very well get you into trouble: *revolt, wretched, rhesus, riot, rot, rendezvous.* She later would wish that she had thought to say the word *monster* begins with *M.* And how safe a sort of word is that?

LESSON 40

How can we ever travel together?
Wie können wir da jemals miteinander reisen?

———

Was the zookeeper handsome? Was Amalie exquisite?

Through summer and into the dark days of autumn, they met at the zoo or his apartment. She with handbag and heels. She with hair knotted into a knot at her nape. She was to him the pinnacle of civilization. And the absolute white flag of its discontents.

How did he get that curious limp?

She called him Lou. He said not to. She called him Louis. He said, *Don't.* She called him Louie, he said, *Stop.* She asked him, *Well what should I call you?* He said, *Don't.* And she laughed and laughed.

Did she love him?

A chimpanzee poacher shot Louis Apollinaire.

Where exactly is the wild to be found these days?

She did not yet know, as she waited for him on the bench on that afternoon in 1976, as the rain began to fall, as she sat pondering the virtues and vices of monsters, that she was going to have a second child.

Did he love her?

Through the days of that dismal summer that she believed in some manner they owned, the window by his bed stayed jammed

III

open with a green soda bottle. The fire department sent out men to turn on the hydrants and let the city kids splash in the cold water. And she heard them in the street laughing. She watched from the window. The yellow curtains fluttered. A small fan turned the air. There was a clock on the wall. The hands of the clock did not move. No, no, this cannot be true; the hands of the clock must have moved, must move, clockwise, even in her memory. It was only that she could not see the movement, the incremental accumulation, the heaping up and loss of time. The telephone did not ring. The clock did not glow in the dark. The hands did not move. Two stained coffee cups unwashed in the sink. They drank coffee, black and unsweetened, cooked up in a little Cuban pot on a hot plate. She fell asleep during the bright hot afternoon and when she awoke: darkness. She did not care about time. And yet the moment that she awoke in the darkness she knew that it was time to go home. There must be a finite past, shut down, locked up, boarded over, closed like the zoo concession stand in December.

How does it end? Does it end badly?

With his dark curls going to silver and his sun-savaged face, he was trapped between the sumptuous descriptors: *rugged* and *fragile*. He in the bed watched her dress; the heat had not broken. She was *elegant*, yet *sturdy*. She ran a brush through her blonde hair before pulling it against her hand into a knot and knotting it around itself; before putting on her shoes and picking up her purse and heading home to her husband and son.

Why didn't they run away together?

1976 passed. It became as useless as 1776. New Halloween costumes were devised: Luke Skywalker and Princess Leia; Fonzi and Farrah; R2-D2 and C-3PO. No more Pocahontas; good-bye to Paul Bunyan. Birds pecked at seeds, the fallen bread, the oyster crackers, hot dog buns scattered into bits around the iron bench where Amalie Leopold used to sit. The ash of fallen cigarettes dispersed. New girls worked at the concession stand, but they wore the same yellow smocks. When the weather turned cold, the girls buttoned cardigan sweaters over their uniforms. When the manager wasn't around, they cracked jokes and spied on adulterers and ate salted peanuts warm from the shell. Good-bye Snoopy and Charlie Brown. Good-bye Louis and Amalie. And Lewis and Clark. The sky darkened in October. November was brittle. December: mournful. Where were the jokes? The nonsense words? Frankenstein and Dracula? The gobbledygook, the snickerdoodle, the Homo sapiens and hullabaloo alike? Good-bye zookeeper! Good-bye Mrs. Leopold. After he was gone and there was no more of him, Amalie joined a society to raise money for rain-forest preservation. She collected funds for animal shelters. She helped find homes for animals retired from the circus. Her image of him changed shape. He was what and who and wherever she wanted him to be. Every time a skull or bone was discovered in a riverbed and touted in the newspapers as one more piece of the missing link, she knew that he was the practical joker behind it. She saw him holding the shovel. She saw on television a news story about a Siberian tiger who escaped from a Las Vegas stage show and found his way to the desert, where searchers lost his trail. In film footage the tiger wore a fez and red-sequined vest. He was jumping through a hoop of fire. Mrs. Leopold sat with the zookeeper until it began to rain. Soon it would be 1977. When the rain slanted and crosswise fell fine upon them, she folded up her magazine into her handbag, straightened her scarf, smoothed her skirt, and she left him. He sat for a while after she was gone. And the rain fell and fell. Even the concession-stand girls paused over their bags of peanuts to ponder the darkness.

What about right and wrong?

Whom can such a question help?

What about the concession-stand girls?

The first girl's name was Jennifer. Evangeline came in later and opened the second window. The girls drank orange soda and ate peanuts; they watched, and made up stories about, the zookeeper with the cane and the blonde-haired lady. Jenny said that it was a torrid affair. But Evy was a romantic; she said that the two were obviously in love.

Why was Mrs. Leopold so indiscreet?

Those fine things that had once been important to her were worn thin and threadbare; and hope itself was going the way of the Peter Pan collar, the pilgrim dress, and the pedal pusher. What one believed or did not believe was as variable as the height of a hemline. One had to keep up. One had to think about *now*. Even if *now* was *vulgar*. When it was gone, she would miss it. Just as she would miss the zookeeper. She would miss the vulgarity of the new age.

Was Dr. Leopold aware of his wife's indiscretions?

Dr. and Mrs. Leopold, married fully fifteen years, had matching tables of blonde wood on each side of their impressively large bed in their spacious wall-to-wall-carpeted bedroom. On each table was a matching lamp. A telephone and an alarm clock sat on the doctor's table. The telephone rang at odd hours. There were emergencies. There were in the world even late at night sick cats and suffering dogs. You could not fault the importance of Dr. Leopold's work. The clock glowed in the dark. Lives were in the habit, now and again, of needing to be saved.

What about Ben?

Benjamin Leopold, called Benjy, born in November 1965, was a child preoccupied with the concept of time. He possessed the worrisome sense that he was forgetting each moment as it happened. This led to certain anxieties and literal inclinations. The ineluctable *now* forever eluded him. If he gave up thinking about the moment he was in, it would too soon become the past; and first *the moment* and then even *the memory of the moment* might be lost to him.

What happened to Jenny and Evangeline?

After Evy quit, Jenny never had as much fun working with anyone else. Jenny lasted through to the next July. She grew tired of working for a manager who forever refused to order and stock enough Bomb Pops. They always ran out of Bomb Pops. And she had to make signs on notebook paper: OUT OF BOMB POPS! SORRY! But she wasn't sorry.

If every July the concession stand ran out of red, white, and blue Bomb Pops, why didn't the manager learn from history and order more?

The manager had grown to anticipate the drama of running out of Bomb Pops. Every year there was a chance that things might be different. Every year could not possibly be the same. Things, he was certain, would balance out. Maybe next July exactly no one will want a Bomb Pop. It will be a delirium of root beer floats.

The baby was?

Named Louisa, but called Lemon.

Why was she called Lemon?

Mrs. Leopold, call her Amy, once won a contest at a public swimming pool on a very hot day in the summer of 1954. She held her breath underwater longer than any other boy or girl splashing in the water on that August afternoon.

What does that mean?

Maybe there is a chance that Louis Apollinaire will not leave Mrs. Leopold. Maybe events are not fixed, fastened, and glued, bolted down in time. Maybe cosmic passion is in their lucky stars. After all, it is difficult enough to figure out what has already happened, let alone to imagine a future. Best not to become too giddy with the promise of happiness, nor sad, sentimental, or suspect at the worm-turning revisions of fate. Why do children love the monkey house? What did Benjy remember? Where are the concession-stand girls now, years later? What has become of their smocks? What happened to the baby in the blue crocheted hat who stared up at the sky? Did the birds, the brown, the black, the little, the big, survive that winter? And the next? And the one after? Better to live like Mrs. Leopold on an October afternoon as she waits for rain, as she waits for Louis Apollinaire, with the idea of possibility, if not possibility itself.

LESSON 41

She finds red currants too sour without sugar
Johannisbeeren sind ihr ohne Zucker zu sauer

———

Pick one moment out of the past and replay it endlessly.

LESSON 42

That joke really made us laugh
Wir haben über diesen Witz sehr gelacht

———

Elsa believed that the German people wanted to kill her.

LESSON 43

You have to draw the next card
Du musst die nächste Karte ziehen

———

Upon the horsehair sofa she reclined. Elsa in Dr. Apfel's inner office.

The doctor sat in his chair with his back to the window. He smoked his pipe. It was a windy autumn afternoon. The garden gate had not been fastened properly, and it now and again banged open and closed.

Elsa cradled her arm.

The doctor was silent.

The girl said, *A blind man asks a lame beggar, "How do you get along?" And the beggar replies, "As you see."*

Elsa was glad to be out of her house. For her mother was cleaning from top to bottom; Mother didn't trust the maid to clean properly, thoroughly; to clean with devotion.

There were no clocks in the doctor's room. Dark floral papered the walls. A tea table. Glass-domed lamps. She sat upon the sofa. The shelves held curios, statues, and stone tablets. The Persian rug with tasseled edges upon the wooden floor. Here slept the dog undeterred by his own or Elsa's dreams. The drawn-back curtains revealed, through the leaded-glass panes of the window, the garden: wind wracked the rose vines and the bare limbs of the plum trees. Open and closed went the gate. It was not an unpleasant room. Closed and closed, she curled her feet beneath her on the sofa. Rain pattered against the panes.

Why was Mother so compelled to scrub the floors, the walls, and the windows?

Father was Karl. And mother was Frederika.

Father, ever so clever, as a young man had worked with accounts in the office of a button factory in the town of D—; he married the pretty daughter of his factory owner. Frederika, ten years younger than her husband, bore her first daughter at nineteen. Her next three children followed in quick succession. Karl inherited the factory; he moved his family to Berlin. For Father hated small towns and longed for a cosmopolitan life. Frederika began to suffer some rather *unspeakable* feminine problems. When Elsa was eight, her father had taken ill with nervous exhaustion; the family moved briefly from Berlin to live in the spa town of W—; it was here that they made the acquaintance of a young married couple, the Kaufmanns. Frau Magda Kaufmann, plump and adorable, befriended Karl Z. And afternoons while Frederika took mud cures for relief of her *unspeakable* ailments, Frau Magda tended to Elsa's father in his room. They kept the door locked.

Elsa was not sweet-tempered like her sister Berit, nor as efficient as Martha. And while Elsa had been such a smart little girl, as far as little girls go, she was not like her brother, Theodor, the bright hope for the family's future. At ten Theodor went to school at the Gymnasium, where he was to prepare for the University and where he would learn, among so many other impressive things, to read the *Odyssey* in Greek. Martha, Berit, and Elsa continued to study at home with a governess. Theodor had left Elsa behind; and she was miserable. Later she went to a convent day school.

Father had a fondness for the governess, who had taught the girls grammar, piano, and manners. And he had a fondness for the maid. And although Elsa was uncertain—yes, she thought, her father was rather fond of the cook as well.

Mother was pretty, but shrill and brittle. And Father, charming, but callous.

Martha was sensible. Berit: beautiful. Theodor was everyone's favorite, except for Martha, who could not conceal her jealousy.

Martha had a son named Stefan. And Berit had a baby boy named Frederik. Elsa despised the spoiled Stefan but was ambivalent about Fredi. Both boys had been baptized. Both of her sisters and their husbands had converted from Judaism to Christianity. Mother had been baptized as well. And even Father had become—though he said it was only for the sake of his business—Christian. Mother said it was only practical.

Mother thought she was practical, but she was not.

Elsa had not been baptized. She found religion silly; just as silly as trying to change what you are or were by saying a magic word like *abracadabra*. Mother was forever getting at Elsa now about the state of the girl's soul. What is less practical than a soul?

Elsa looked around the room.

There were paintings; framed postcards; a collection of wing-pinned butterflies.

Elsa often was asked to watch over Käthe and Greta Kaufmann, the two little daughters of Otto and Magda. Herr Kaufmann was most appreciative of Elsa's attentions to his children.

Magda Kaufmann had an adorable white body.

Father thought he was discreet, but he was not.

Elsa had come in through the back garden gate. She was the one who had left the latch undone and now it rattled, open and closed.

She saw—she could see—who was it? Franz in his woolen coat—he must have come around from the kitchen way—to fasten closed the gate. And he stood in the raw darkening afternoon, waiting, leaning against the far stone wall—tangled with rose vines—in the rain.

LESSON 44

The doctor informed her of the risks of the operation
Der Arzt informierte sie über die Risiken der Operation

———

How do we know what we know?

Anna, in the manner of little girls in big houses, overheard more than anyone suspected.

Anna had questions.

What went on in Father's rooms?

To whom did Maman write her letters?

Why did Franz stand in the rain by the roses?

Anna listened at the closed door of Father's inner office.

Are dreams the royal road to the unconscious?

Does existence precede essence?

What walks on four legs at dawn; and two legs at noon; and three legs at night?

What will become of us?

On the stairs Anna overheard.

From the doorway she saw.

In the kitchen Dolfi taught Franz how to bake cakes.

Franz, with shirtsleeves rolled, untied the looping knot of Dolfi's apron.

Dolfi had eyes of cocoa brown; her skin was like a creamy egg custard.

Franz delighted in dough. Dolfi taught him how to knead. And he was an intent student to her round arms. But Dolfi's instructions ended at the oven.

It was Tulla, the maid, who taught him other lessons.

Tulla had freckles. And when she laughed, she threw back her head.

Tulla wound her ginger-red plaits up and up and round and round with her quick fingers.

Tulla had had her share of kisses from the doctor's son.

She loved poor dear Franz, she did.

And she would never deny him anything that he asked.

He came to her in her little room in the attic.

She undid her stockings.

She unwound her plaits.

And then Franz stopped going to Tulla for kisses.

He stopped untying Dolfi's apron.

Franz grew sad; he became distant.

He did not in the kitchen roll dough.

He was restless, and he paced about the garden.

He smoked cigarettes.

Ashes on the stone path.

Anna sat between Tulla and Dolfi at the kitchen table.

Anna was drawing upon a scrolling roll of paper.

Tulla said to Dolfi: *Do you suppose that Franz is in love with me?*

Dolfi said: *No, no. If he's in love then it's awful. It must be an awful kind of love.*

Tulla's feelings were bruised; why shouldn't Franz have fallen for her?

Just then there was a knock at the door.

It was Aron come round from the butcher's with his bloody bundles tied with twine. Such magnificent *Wurst!* It made Tulla go hungry with laughter to see such lovelies strung up and dangling fat, silly, salty, and delicious in shop windows.

Tulla told Dolfi, *I'll see to Aron.*

Aron whistled and sang and never failed to bring a soup bone for the dog.

Dolfi looked at Anna's drawing.

Is that our house? Dolfi said. *Aren't you clever! Isn't it perfect!*

Anna sat between Tulla and Dolfi as they joked over jam.

What did Anna want to know?

How do you know what you want?

Cake, the cat, licked clean a plate.

Franz in love, sighed Dolfi. *What will happen next?*

His heart will be broken, said Tulla.

Tulla's heart kept accurate time.

Tulla knew what was what.

When she could slip away, she went with Aron to his room above the butcher shop.

She knew how to keep out of trouble; but if the worst came down to it, which it did not because she was ever so clever with tricks and remedies; there were places where girls with *that* problem could go. Still *it* never happened to *her;* but she had heard stories. Stories that she told to Dolfi, whose wide eyes widened in her plump face, oh! Stories that Anna—as she sat at the kitchen table peeling potatoes—collected into memory.

In such a way, we learn what is what.

LESSON 45

The policeman ran after the thief
Der Polizist lief dem Dieb nach

Upon the bed in her hotel room. Lemon in silk pajamas.

She called Ben on her cell phone.

"Tell me about Berlin," he said.

"The food is awful," she said. "And such large portions."

She said, "Have you heard this one? A psychiatrist runs into a long-lost friend and says, 'I heard that you died!' The friend says, 'Ah! But you see I'm alive.' 'Impossible!' says the psychiatrist, 'The man who told me is much more reliable than you.'"

"I don't get it," said Ben.

"Did I tell it wrong?" she said.

"Maybe I told it wrong," she said.

She said, "A man goes to see his psychiatrist. He says, 'Doctor, Doctor, last night I had the strangest dream. I dreamed that I saw my mother at a party. She was wearing a white dress, and when she turned around to look at me, she had your face. I woke up and couldn't get back to sleep. I just lay there in bed, waiting for morning. Finally, morning came. I got up, drank a coke, and rushed right over for my appointment, so that I could ask you: what does it mean?'"

"What does the doctor say?" said Ben.

"He says, 'A coke? *That* you call breakfast?'" said Lemon.

"That doesn't answer my question," he said.

"What question?" she said.

He said, "Poor Lemon."

"Don't 'Poor Lemon' me," she said.

"Poor Lemon *you,*" she said.

"What about Anna?" he said.

"I can't hear you," she said.

"—Anna?" he said. "She's real?"

"She's ninety," said Lemon. "What's more *real* than that?"

He asked, "Has she told you the story?"

"She's telling it," she said.

He said, "You've been there for—"

She said, "I feel like I've been here forever. I feel like I've never been anywhere else."

He said, "Did you ask her why she wants to tell the story *now?*"

"Oh," said Lemon. "Isn't it obvious?"

"No," said Ben.

"You really take the cake," said Lemon.

"What?" said Ben.

"It's a joke," said Lemon.

"Is it?" he said.

"Do you believe her?" said Ben.

"What does it matter," she asked, "what I believe?"

"Now who's deep?" he said.

"What?" she said.

"What sort of proof do you need?" she asked.

"Be scientific," he said. "Be objective."

Lemon said. "Do you want to hear the craziest thing? Anna said that the doctor's first wife, Klara—could see ghosts. And that Franz inherited it from his mother. Franz saw ghosts too, and it drove him crazy. And these are not, you know, *metaphorical*—or is it *metaphysical?*—But real flesh-and-bone ghosts. That's our great-grandmother,

and then our grandfather. Have you heard—do you remember—
when you were little—did you ever hear anything about—?"

"Ghosts?" he said.

"I know, I know," she said. "Not only don't you believe in ghosts,
you aren't even frightened of them. But is it true?"

"I thought you were beyond caring about something as *artificial*
as truth—" he said.

"I've never seen a ghost," she said. "Have you?"

"Why do you have a German accent?" he asked.

"I don't," she said. "Do I?"

"You tell me," he said.

There was silence on the line.

"How are you?" she suddenly asked.

"If you could find proof—" he said.

"Eliza says she's done with love stories," said Lemon.

"What?" he said.

"Even stopped clocks are right twice a day," she said.

The connection crackled out.

LESSON 46

Oh my heavens, I can only drive an automatic!
Ach du lieber Himmel, ich kann nur automatische Schaltung fahren!

———

When she was eighteen-years-old and maybe naïve and improbably innocent, Eliza saw Hart Luther for the first time. She was walking from the library when she changed her path and cut through to the courtyard; she found herself in the courtyard where students were gathered to watch the man in the bell tower. She remembered; she summoned from memory the image of that day. The white ice skates slung over the shoulder of the girl in the ski jacket. The girl's name was Rennie. The girl with the white ice skates tugged at Hart's sleeve. If Eliza replayed the scene again perhaps she could find it; the thing that had led her to Hart.

It was not *the thing* itself, but *the absence of the thing*.

It was not Hart, but the lack of him.

It was not the way the body fell from the bell tower; it was not the lack of a crash of bone upon brick that caused consternation in the students down below. It was not the lie. It was the absence of the truth.

That fall semester someone kept calling in bomb threats on the girls' dormitories.

The bomb threats were the supposed work of radical student activists.

One never knew what a radical student activist would do.

So there was a training exercise on a day in January.

What if there were a man in the bell tower with a gun?

But there was no man in the bell tower with a gun.

Eliza hurled a bottle, and it hit a police car. And then she turned and ran. It was not the bottle that mattered. The bottle was glass. The falling body was not real. The sky was gray. She had looked up toward that cloudy gray Midwestern sky, swollen with the possibility of snow.

Pick one moment from the past and live within it until the memory begins to generate its own set of outcomes distinctly different from what really happened.

What really happened?

The moment was the thing. No, no, it was not *the thing* itself but *the persistence of the absence of that moment.* She could recall: the laces of the skates tied into neat looping knots. Someone went to get binoculars. The sound of the shot. The body as it fell. The dull thud with which it hit the courtyard. The darkening sky—so early—of a January afternoon. The training exercise had been scheduled during the holiday break. It was just after New Year's; students were not supposed to be hanging around campus. But Eliza was walking home from work at the library; and Hart Luther had a girlfriend called Rennie who wanted to go ice skating.

Pick a moment out of the past and replay it endlessly.

Things should have been different.

Could things have been different?

But because Eliza had changed her path and cut across and through the courtyard, and because Hart and Rennie had gotten into an argument and the girl had grabbed her skates and stormed out of his apartment and he had followed after, the three of them ended up together in the courtyard just as the sharpshooter from the nearby window of the physics building shot the dummy down from the bell tower.

Rennie said, *Doesn't that just take the cake!*

Was the cake the thing that needed to be taken?

Eliza was, of course, free to remember it any way that she liked. She could change the order and outcome of events; how she first saw him. How they did not really *meet* on that day.

She could imagine that the sun broke through the clouds.

It did not.

She could envision: the girl with the ice skates leaving without Hart.

But Rennie did not.

Eliza could dream that Hart saw her hurl the bottle at the police car and that he fell in love with her at that moment.

Hart did not.

Hart Luther did not believe in love.

Don't you remember what he used to say?

Love is terrorism.

The next time Eliza saw Hart, he was standing before her at the library circulation desk waiting to check out *Jokework* by Dr. Jozef Apfel.

Eliza held onto the book for a moment too long before handing it back to him, and she suddenly blurted out, *Do you remember when that body fell from the tower?*

And he looked at her.

And he said with surprise, *Oh? Were you there?*

LESSON 47

What was the motive for the crime?
Was war der Beweggrund des Verbrechens?

———————

Hart Luther's great-grandfather was an actor in a traveling theatrical troupe. He called no place home, and no one, in later years, knew from where exactly he had come. He told stories about his childhood in Spain, in Egypt, in the Garden of Eden, in America, in a village so deep in the heart of the Pale it had a name that could not be spoken. He walked in a blinding snowstorm from St. Petersburg to Paris—barefoot—in barely three days time; he swore to this. In Cordoba he grew up concealing his religion and eating apricots in the sun. No, no, it didn't happen that way. It went like this: he ran rum, guns, and wild with the Purple Gang in Detroit. While he was bathing in the Nile, the famous talking cat of Luxor stole his clothes from the shore. In Buenos Aires on the steps of the opera house, Toscanini tipped his top hat and tossed him a coin for luck. It was all true. Or maybe none of it was. Avram Hertz, the vagabond actor, was a liar. But his lies were dreams, and his dreams were monumental things; each one an ocean voyage away from the small Galician towns to and from which a team of beleaguered dray horses pulled the troupe's overloaded wagon. He fell in love with a young actress called Eve Emmeline. And when she gave birth to a son, Avram Hertz said the boy had been delivered of his line-laboring mother on stage as Ophelia during Act IV of *Hamlet,* but the incomparable Eve

Emmeline insisted that a gaggle of white geese dropped the baby into her lap at midnight on the road to Lublin. And though those two wholehearted homeless dreamers, Avram and Eve, never married, don't judge or despair; after all, did not God tell them to be fruitful and multiply?

The boy was named Wolf. And in succession followed sisters, Mathilde and Sofie; and then brothers, Oskar, Elias, and Heinrich. The actors went on performing comedy and tragedy alike, and when an infant was needed for a scene, they were very lucky indeed, because they could use a real child rather than a doll. As the children grew, they played all manner of characters, from animals to dwarves to demons. In a Lemburg production of *A Midsummer Night's Dream*, young Wolf stole the show as Puck. Tarnapol Minor would remember always his wicked portrayal of the Grimms' Rumpelstiltskin. His last role in his father's troupe was an uproariously coy Vashti in a Purim pageant; when he removed his veil to reveal the beginnings of a beard, the audience went wild with laughter. At sixteen, Wolf Hertz fought in the Great War on the Italian front. He said he escaped a prison camp. He said he walked right through the front gates and waved good-bye to the guards. He said they threw kisses, calling out to him: *In bocca al lupo!* He said he tunneled out using a stick, a spoon, and a potato. He said he lost a toe to gangrene. He said he stowed away on a merchant ship, and when he was discovered, he was thrown overboard. He said he rode the fierce blue Aegean on the back of a whale. He said that Greek fishermen casting out their nets had rescued him. He made his way by ship and whale and tale to Palestine. And there he saw only the past—sand and ruins; stones and smashed idols—everywhere he looked. He found work in a factory that bottled soda pop. The serials, dime novels, and pulp stories that he devoured during those hot dry desert days taught him English. Westerns were his favorite—Zane Grey, of course, and his purple sage—but he admired the elegantly unfortunate opium addict, Zenith the Albino, and he followed in *Thriller Weekly* the capers of Blackshirt, the gentleman crook. What happened next? In 1922 Wolf Hertz made his way to Constantinople and sailed steerage via Smyrna, Piraeus, and Messina on that once exquisite ocean liner, *Regina d'Italia*. When he arrived at Ellis Island, he was twenty-one years old. *Hertz* was only a memory; *Luther* was the new name that he gave himself.

From New York Wolf Luther made his way west, crossed the country mile by acre, lured by the promise of California—only to find, when he finally arrived—another desert. He couldn't resist Hollywood. He landed roles—Indians, cowboys, sultans, bandits, buccaneers, and bank robbers—as an extra in the silents. More than once he wore the striped pajamas and leg irons of an escaped convict. He said that for a while he was rolling in the dough-ray-mee; he made a bundle betting on the ponies; paled around poolside with Pola Negri at the Argyle Hotel; tossed plot lines to Irving Thalberg; drove the Stutz Bearcat of an amorous aging starlet; and ran tight with a gang of tough guys smuggling booze from Mexico. He might have stayed on, made his home in the Hollywood Hills, but when he read in the papers that Houdini had died in a Detroit hospital, it broke his heart. If the great escape artist could succumb to a sucker punch to the stomach, what chance was there for less limber Jews? Wolf Luther lingered down and dissolute through one more sunny winter, working at bit parts with dispassion, keeping mostly to himself, reading Jules Verne novels, and fermenting Vine-go grape jelly into wine. And when he headed back East, it was in style; he bought a first-class ticket from Los Angeles to Chicago on the Golden State Limited, which ran the rails under the exquisitely futile promise: *every mile in comfort.* He stepped off the air-conditioned train and walked out of the station into the thick heat of Midwestern summer. And marveled at the sprawling downtown. Louis B. Mayer himself couldn't have dreamed a better city than Chicago: mad for baseball; corrupt to the core; angle-angling gangsters and thugs and immigrants crowding the streets; beautiful girls sitting at lunch counters; everywhere the smell of sweat and smoke and gin and rot and hot dogs; and the great barges rolling and chuffing along the green water of Lake Michigan. Mark Twain called Berlin, "the German Chicago," but that has nothing to do with this part of the story. Suffice it to say: Wolf Luther, formerly Hertz, never went back, as he had planned, to the LaSalle Street Station to catch the 20th Century eastward to New York. Instead, he worked—a union agitator, shoe salesman, orderly in a mental ward, short-order cook—rambling from job to job until he landed a steady gig doing sound effects for radio soap operas. He married a girl named Sylvie, and they had four sons; the third was called Harry. Harry Luther did not have the theatrical flair that had driven his grandfather to the stage and his own father to travel under an assumed name from one desert to the next to end up smack in the middle of America. Harry Luther became an accountant, and he was happy for the protective anonymity of his surname in a place where it was the opposite of uncommon. The telephone book was rife with *Luther*s. Who was to say they were not all fugitive Jews? And, who, after all, cared to recall or recollect anymore the myriad woes of the Old World? Harry Luther had a son named Hart. And Hart Luther in turn inherited, in more and doubled, every dark and dreamy and dramatic longing that his own father had not.

LESSON 48

If everything else fails
Wenn alle Stricke reissen

———≈———

Enjoy Berlin.

Rent a car. Take a day trip. Drive as fast as you like.

Visit a spa. For all that ails you there is a remedy. Take the mineral waters. Indulge in a full body massage, mud facial, salt bath, high colonic irrigation, or seaweed wrap. Get your hair done. Be beautiful. Be handsome.

Be brave and fantastic.

Imagine that your life is a movie.

Pretend that you are a character in a movie.

Treat yourself. Go to a nice restaurant. Eat sushi, falafel, *Milchreis* and *Currywurst*. For dessert they will bring coffee and anything else that you want: *Blitzkuchen mit Äpfeln; Pfeffernüsse; Bayerische Erdbeercreme; Bienenstich.* Perhaps a *Schwarzwälder Kirschtorte?* Viennese caramel cream was Hitler's favorite. He stood before the map and announced: *We now have to face the task of cutting up the giant cake according to our needs.*

He planned to dominate the world with *pastry and whip!*

What kind of cake did he imagine on the plate?

Pretend that you are German.

LESSON 49

It is estimated that about thirty percent of waste can be recycled
Es wird geschätzt, dass rund dreissig prozent des Mülls
wiederverwertet werden kann

———

Ben did not go to Berlin.

He was sitting by the pool reading a script. It was called *Faust*. It was a modern (no, no, post-) telling of the classic tale. In this version of the story, Faust was a down-in-the-count baseball player, who is offered the chance to change his fate by a mobster menacingly called Mephisto. Lemon had been offered the role of Gretchen, the good-hearted dance hall moll.

The swimming pool shimmered in the moonlight.

It was now too dark to read.

Ben thought that the script was awful; but as it went on, scene by scene, he found himself, despite himself, wanting to know what would happen next.

LESSON 50

What did Miss Braun bring?
Was brachte Fräulein Braun mit?

⟨⟨⟨

Elsa said.

Father had syphilis.

Mother was frigid.

Berit gorged on cream cakes and then made herself vomit.

Martha was mean-spirited and malicious.

Theodor wrote Communist pamphlets marshaling factory workers to rise up against the oppressions of management. He distributed his pamphlets to the workers in father's factory.

Elsa confessed: they had never been a happy family.

She complained about the stares of strangers.

Why did they glare at her?

Why did they whisper as she passed on the street?

What did they know that she did not?

How did they *know?*

Elsa: her head hurt. And her arm: she cradled it like a child.

Lugged it like a brick. Held it; hoped for it; fussed; coddled; complained; forced it heavy and numb into her blouse, coaxed it from her coat sleeve. Pulled on her gloves finger by finger as a girl would dress a favorite doll.

Father kept a mistress. Mother was a shrew. Father was a tyrant. Mother wanted *to make memories;* and what could be more stupid than that? Mother had tried to force the children to believe that they were happy. Martha spoiled little Stefan to the point of impossibility. The boy bullied, demanded, commanded, and carried on like an undersized emperor! Berit cared only about the fashion of the latest dresses from Paris, and let her baby cry in the arms of his nursemaid. Theodor was lucky; he was faraway now. He would not come home even when his mother begged. Elsa was not the prettiest of the girls, said Mother. Elsa was not the smartest of the children, said Father.

Father was a brute.

He smashed plates.

Mother was selfish.

She shrieked.

Martha bragged.

Berit simpered.

Theodor ran and hid.

The doctor listened while Elsa let her thoughts take her where they may.

When Elsa was thirteen—just before the war—the Kaufmanns had rented a house for the summer in O———. Where the waters—mineral springs—were known for their restorative tonic. Berit was to be married, and Mother and Frau Magda Kaufmann suddenly became dear friends, joined in their delight over planning the wedding. What a jolly party they had made going to the summer house: Frau Madga K. and Frau Frederika Z., along with Martha and her little Stefan, and Berit, the beautiful, the almost bride. Elsa had stayed on in Berlin with Father. But then Berit had turned her ankle walking in the woods. And the ladies cut short their holiday and traveled back to the city because Frau Z. worried that Berit should consult a city physician—for who could trust a country doctor?—lest she be lamed for life. Frau Magda, leaving her two daughters in the care of the housekeeper, had returned to Berlin with them. And Elsa had been dispatched by train to O——— to see to the Kaufmann girls.

How nice that had been for while: Elsa played and roamed and picked wildflowers with little Käthe and Greta. But then Herr K. arrived back from a business trip. He praised her for watching the children; he brought her gifts: an album of picture postcards, a string of painted beads, a silk scarf, a box of sweets. Days passed in idyll. Herr K. confided in her. He whispered. He embraced her. He called her his little wife. And said that all families should be as happy as the four of them were together that summer. He kissed her; playfully, as Father might. It was all a game, wasn't it? And how the sun brightened her pale skin; how she laughed chasing after Käthe and Greta, hiding and seeking; though Elsa warned them not to go too deep into the woods. And then one evening Otto K. found her when she was alone, away from the girls. He grew forward. He kissed: roughly. He demanded: ingraciously. He pleaded: longingly. How long must he suffer? How long would she make him wait? He promised her impossibilities that stirred if not her heart then her vengeance. He would leave his wife for her! He would abandon Magda—oh! The minx, fickle, cruel; he knew that she was the mistress of Elsa's father! Magda was faithless and cold—if only his dear little Elsa would say the word!

What was the word?

The idea was not without temptation to Elsa.

Wouldn't it show Father that everyone knew about his mistress? Wouldn't it just gall Mother and Martha and Berit, who mocked Elsa for being already a spinster at heart? Wouldn't it say something to haughty Magda that a child as meek and nervous as Elsa could steal her husband away? Elsa dreamed—to be sure. But vengeance was good for little else. She could not imagine being a bride. She could not imagine a life with Herr K. She wanted to escape her family, not to become more entangled. She would run away; she would get away—hide from them—just as Theodor had—at the first chance.

Greta and Käthe had fine pretty faces. Elsa tucked the girls into their bed at night; and they held Elsa's hands one on each side as

139

they ran along the forest's dark pine-fringed edges. They grew tan. They grew sturdy. They would grow up.

What would become of them?

Father was always right.

Mother was beautiful.

Martha: assured and capable.

Berit: quick with needle and thread.

Theodor: full of brilliant ideas.

Asked Elsa: *What will become of us, Doctor?*

Summer ended.

The evenings grew cold; the leaves on the larch trees turned dark and red-russet.

And then one evening when the girls and the housekeeper had gone to a carnival, Herr K. found Elsa picking wildflowers; she had promised the girls to help dry and press the blooms in the pages of a memory book. There was a little cottage nearby. He pressed her against the whitewashed building. He tore her dress. She reached out and slapped his face. He grabbed her by the wrist. He held her. She called out; but no one lingered, no one passed; the summer folk all had gone to the carnival. She pleaded with Herr K. She begged. She fought. He would not be stopped. He cried out: *You mustn't say no, you must never say no!*

And she could hear the music from the bandstand.

What pity even then, as he pinned her wrists, she felt for him.

Afterwards he kissed me; he held my hand. We went together to the carnival. He told funny stories as we walked, she said. *He joked. He said: Louis XV wanted to test the wit of one of his courtiers of whose talent he had been told. At the first opportunity he commanded the gentleman to tell a joke of which he, the king, should be the subject. The courtier at once made the clever reply: "Ah, but the king is never the subject!"*

Said Elsa: *Last night I dreamed the branches were cut from the lime trees; I saw the vines dry and bare. I saw a girl standing before a tombstone. She looked at me from over her shoulder; she held out to me her hands, palms open and empty. I dreamed that seven hungry calves ate seven fine fat-well-fleshed calves. I dreamed that I was as happy as an American.*

And? asked the doctor.

Then I woke up, she said.

Dr. Apfel wanted to hear more about Elsa's tryst with Herr Kaufmann, whom he knew to be upstanding and handsome. He wanted to know why a girl would fight off and refuse the advances of a dashing gentleman who was so smitten with her?

Who said I refused? said Elsa.

LESSON 51

Manfred gave me a bunch of red carnations
Manfred hat mir einen Strauss roter Nelken geschenkt

———

When Elsa came back from the summer house, Magda teased her.
Did you fall in love with my Otto? she had asked.
Magda knew everything.
Wasn't it a thrill?
What a lark!
Such a wonderful naughty way to spend a holiday.
Wasn't Elsa lucky to have Magda looking out for her?
It had been Magda's idea. She had made certain that Otto and Elsa would be left alone together. Of course, she couldn't take all the credit. Otto really did adore Elsa.
And even Father had agreed to it.
Father knew.
Karl would do anything for Magda.
Upstairs Madame Madeline was at the piano. And in the kitchen Dolfi was baking tarts.
Magda had kept Mother distracted with Berit's wedding plans so that Elsa could be naughty with Otto. Wasn't it a wicked caper?
Elsa clasped at her head with her one hand.
The piece that Madame was playing ended abruptly.
Elsa told this joke to the doctor:
A man went on a journey and left his daughter in the care and household of a friend with the strict orders that the friend must guard

the beautiful girl's virtue. Some months later when the man returned, he found that his daughter was pregnant. He approached his friend, who was unable to explain the misfortune. "Well," asked the father, "where did my daughter sleep?" The friend replied, "In the same room as my son, of course." The father said, "How could you let her share a room with your son?" The friend protested, saying, "But there was a screen placed between their two beds!" The father said, "And suppose the boy walked around the screen?" The friend pondered. He replied thoughtfully, "Yes, there is that. It might have happened like that."

Upstairs at the piano Madame Madeline resumed with a waltz.

What was I saying? asked Elsa. *Oh yes. I came home from the summer house.*

She came home. Magda teased Elsa. *Do you love my husband?* she asked. Magda was a great reader of crime stories. Magda and Elsa were mad for the cinema. Magda Kaufmann imagined that if Frau Z. were to take with an accident, then she might be free to marry Herr Z. And Elsa could marry Herr K., and what jolly fun they would all have then! Of course, she would never do anything to bring about the demise of Elsa's mother. But one never knew what could happen! Accidents! Lightning struck. Hearts stopped. Why, one might eat a poisonous mushroom! One had to imagine the unimaginable. Drama was the spice of life! Magda gobbled torrid romance novels; she had loaned books to Elsa. And when Mother found them, she threw them into the fireplace. Magda got a good laugh out of that. After that, Magda gave the books to Elsa in disguise, with false jackets proclaiming wholesome and instructive stories.

Elsa said that—one afternoon—when returning just such a novel to Frau K.—she walked in on her father and his mistress. Magda Kaufmann, plump and white, naked but for her stockings, in bed—eating chocolates fed to her by Karl Z. *Woof, woof,* Magda cried and she snapped the sweets from Father's fingers like a puppy.

Did Magda really know everything?

Frau Magda did not know everything. Not yet.

But it was to dear devoted Magda that Elsa came with her secret.

Elsa had become the mistress of Herr Otto Kaufmann. And at fifteen she was carrying his child.

LESSON 52

The streets were wet; it must have rained
Die Strassen waren nass; es muss geregnet haben

———

Eliza in a café on the Karl-Marx-Allee.

She was reading a guidebook called *German for Travelers*.

It contained maps, pictures, and a dictionary of phrases. The phrases were meant to be useful. It was hard to imagine going up to a stranger and saying: *Anton looks in the mirror and sees that he is entirely bald.*

Or: *Hands up! I have a revolver!*

Eliza wanted to understand German.

The words, the language, the sentences, the sentiment.

The past was quiet. The café was noisy.

She paged through the book.

She liked to wander. She liked to find her own way.

It was important for her to understand and to be understood.

To learn without being taught.

She wasn't afraid to ask questions.

She followed her heart. She had hope.

And in her heart she was a traveler.

Oh, she had moments of doubt.

She wasn't afraid to admit to moments of doubt.

There were times when the very idea of Germany terrified her.

When the language seemed obscene.

A train chuffing. A dog barking. A devil flying across the sky.

A house in which no one was home.

A clock ticking the wrong time.

Germany: with a romantic history and bright future!

A guidebook for the traveler who wants to understand and in turn, be understood.

For the dreamer who longs to wake.

For the questioner in search of answers.

No declension required: no conjugation necessary.

The scale on the map was set by her measure.

A waiter dropped a plate. It smashed upon the floor. Everyone turned; everyone looked. A girl came by with a broom to sweep up the broken glass. And the clatter of forks and knives and talk at the evening hour resumed.

The plate was real.

For it had smashed.

The forks and knives were real.

Even the spoons.

They were real.

Were they not?

She hated love stories.

But she could not stop writing them.

One after the next.

She was the heroine of her own story.

And a story could and would take a turn for the figurative just when one was feeling so desperately literal. That is—

The more that Eliza saw of Berlin the less real it became to her.

The past was history. And history was a thing. And *the thing* itself was too vague to be grasped or eaten; not like an orange or éclair; not like a ringing telephone or a coffee cup or the pages of a newspaper. The past was ghostly and transparent. It could not be filled in like the squares of a crossword puzzle. Or enjoyed like a bottle of

Coca-Cola. It neither existed nor failed to exist. It had nothing to do with her; with how she wandered or wondered or read useful phrases in her guidebook. It was an abstraction. And yet she was part of this abstraction. It had everything to do with her. History was a joke, sure.

And she was the punch line.

No, the past was not a bar of soap or ink pen.

One symbol replaced another.

She ordered coffee and an éclair.

She paged through the book.

There was a photograph on the cover of two girls at the seaside.

It was not hard to imagine needing to say: *Send for an ambulance!*

LESSON 53

Lotte and Hans are interested in politics
Lotte und Hans interessieren sich für Politik

———

When is a door not a door?
Eliza sat in the café awaiting an éclair.

When it's ajar!
The guidebook belonged to Lemon.

Why is there a fence around the graveyard?
Hart belonged to the past.

Everyone is dying to get in!
Eliza had grown up staring up at the mystery of forward-looking faces in old photographs and wedding portraits that hung by nails upon the floral-papered walls of her home; she was educated among and to adore the secondhand curiosities of her father's store.

What did one skeleton say to the other?
How was it that Hart, the literalist, the loudmouth, the strolling skeleton, the chronic commentator who never said anything that he did not think nor thought anything that he did not say came to fall for a girl like Eliza?

If we had any guts, we'd get out of here!
They met out in the mournful Midwest.

What did one ghost say to the next?

He was checking out a book about jokes by Dr. Jozef Apfel from the library. When she asked him if he remembered the body that fell from the bell tower.

Do you believe in people?

They walked home from the library in the darkness. They crossed the courtyard. He said that she did not look like an American. *What does an American look like?* she asked. He said, *Corn-fed.* He said, *Hog butcher.* He said, *Happy.*

What is the difference between a jeweler and a jailor?

Eliza fell. Figuratively, of course. He talked about what happens in the darkest darkness of forests. He talked about the sale of souls to one devil or another. It grew late. And then it was late. He talked about colonialism, Christianity, and the melting polar ice caps. He talked about maps, apricots, and endangered macaques. He talked about dogs and dyslexia. He said that he read in the newspaper about an unexploded bomb found in a paper bag left in a train station. He wanted to go to Berlin. Accidents do not happen. Nor do they stop happening. He said something about police and thieves. Eliza listened. It is hard to find lost time. They stayed up all night. They talked about tomorrow and the next day.

One sells watches and the other watches cells.

Before going, he kissed her.

What is our nation's greatest problem? The ignorance or the apathy?

They were young. They were good. They were great. They recycled; they reused; they reduced. They visualized world peace. They questioned authority. They told stories at night about travelers. He told her that he longed to travel and to see the world.

I don't know and I don't care!

He was concerned about starvation and baby seals, nuclear waste, deforestation, conservation, germ warfare, jingoism, and justice. But as he worked for and toward an unambiguously better future, he kept turning to look back over his shoulder.

Why are pianos so hard to open?

When the Berlin Wall came down, they watched it on television. *Drop bomb here,* said Hart, pointing to the screen.

Because the keys are inside.

Hart had questions.

What is the best way to call Frankenstein's monster?

Hart could not let the past go. He knew that other causes were more urgent. Dire situations were happening *now*. Famine, flood, disease; the *newest* genocide, the *latest* atrocities. Couldn't he let the grudges and ghosts go? He was bitter; he was beyond reason. What was Germany to him or he to Germany that he should rage so against a world already bombed into the dusty extinction of a textbook's pages? Why did everything come back to Germany? Who had time out in the Midwest to think about Germany? The rain forests were diminishing; the ozone was depleting; the polar ice caps melting. What about global warming? Slavery? Torture? Endangered species? What about the monkeys who had no trees? And trees that had no branches? And branches that bore no fruit? How could Hart ruminate upon Germany? Hart could not help himself. He was haunted by history. A place, a word—a concept—an idea: Germany.

Long distance!

Hart said that everyone had his or her own version of Germany.

Why are cooks so mean?
He said, *Germany is not* Germany *for everyone.*

Because they beat the eggs and whip the butter!
Eliza fell for fanatics.

What did one candle say to the next?
Hart said, *Love is terrorism.*

Let's go out tonight!
Hart said, *Time is tricky.*

Why do birds fly south for the winter?
Hart and Eliza invented a game: Traveler. To invent fate—to go sideways, to shuffle-step, to hop, to hobble, to crabwalk, to jump ahead, to fall back—thwarted time, if only for a little while.

It's too far to walk!
Poor Hart! He bore the weight of so much history on his back.

Where do ghosts live?
Hart was a curiosity. Born too tiny, too early, he had not been expected to survive; the doctors were doubtful. His birth was miraculous. That joke: is there any truth to it? *When you were born your mother said, "What a treasure!" And your father said, "Yes, let's bury it!"* Hart lived. He grew. At times his heart beat too fast. And he ran; he ran to keep pace.

On dead ends!
He was in a hurry.

What kind of lettuce did they serve on the Titanic?

Hart fell for a girl named Berlin. Her name was a place. And a place is never as one imagines it. He fell for her story: for the doctor who dismantled dreams. For the books that lined the library shelves. For butterflies pinned under glass and insects preserved in amber. For jokes and Jews; for what is and what is not. For what was and what will never be. For the knot of her dark hair knotted around itself. For what is manifest and what is destined. He imagined obligation. She dreamed of escape. They invented necessity. And needed nothing else.

Iceberg!

Hart and Eliza did go. Which way did they go? To Germany. To Berlin.

What do you get when you mix a statement with a coat hanger?

They saw such things.

A suspended sentence!

Then one day he died.

Why can't a magician tell his secrets in the garden?

And there was no more of him.

Because the corn are all ears and the potatoes have eyes!

She began writing romance novels.

Which hand is it best to write with?

She wrote book after book as Justine St. Ives. And if Eliza slipped at times into tropes of ropes and roses and the complicated knotty rigging of clipper ships, it was an occupational hazard. She was run off her feet by too much residual sentiment. It was only the by-product—an excess of ether—an overabundance of ardor—of the creation of too many love stories. When overwhelmed by this sweetness, this sickness, this terror, she could not stop herself from looking at the wedding picture of a stunned and serious young couple from the last century: a bride in a black dress holding white flowers, and the groom, Hart Luther, arm in arm, together.

Neither—it's best to write with a pen.
The bitter chocolate éclair arrived, upon a plate. And oh! It was a beautiful thing.

LESSON 54

What time is it?
Wie spät ist es?

In her hotel room.

As Lemon lacquered her nails—

She nibbled on *Schokoladenplätzchen*.

She read an article in *Cosmopolitan* on *creative visualization*.

She saw herself as Elsa Z.

She saw herself as Elsa entering the doctor's house up the snowy garden path and by the kitchen way. Tulla opened the door for her. In the kitchen Dolfi rolled out dough. From upstairs came the sound of Madame at the piano. Lemon as Elsa walked the long corridor. Lemon as Elsa passed the sleeping dog on the polished wooden floor. She passed through the doctor's outer consulting room, with its shelves lined with Greek goddesses and stone tablets; she found the doctor awaiting her in his chair.

She sat upon the tapestry-draped sofa.

She held out her hands to him.

Shadows darkened the doctor's office.

What do you want? the doctor asked the girl.

LESSON 55

At an earlier time, the environment wasn't as polluted as it is today

Früher war die Umwelt noch nicht so verschmutzt wie heute

———

What did Elsa want?

Elsa told Dr. Apfel that Herr Kaufmann had had his way with her.

Do you believe me? she asked.

Does it matter what I believe? he said.

You think that I was in love with him. That I waited for him that night of the carnival. That I seduced him? she said.

Did you? he asked.

Did I? mimicked Elsa.

You were Herr Kaufmann's mistress? said the doctor.

Yes, said Elsa.

And are you still?

No, she said.

Why do you hold your arm like that? he asked.

Like this? she said.

Like a child, he said.

The doctor lighted his pipe.

There wasn't a child, she said.

Elsa had a heart-shaped face and gray eyes with dark brows.

There was a peculiar way that she laughed without laughing.

Said Elsa, *Magda had the whole business taken care of.*

He asked her, *Is something funny?*

She said to the doctor, *There is nothing funny that is not in some way terrible.*

Why do you think that people want to harm you? he asked.

I don't think, she said, *I know it.*

Why? he asked.

Not all people, she said.

Who?

Germans, she said.

How do you know that the Germans want to harm you? he asked.

Not harm, she said. Kill.

He said, *Why do you know that the Germans want to kill you?*

She said, *How do we know what we know?*

She said, *There were once two scheming businessmen, partners, who had amassed a fortune by not altogether scrupulous means. Now that they were rich, they longed to be accepted by high society. To this end they hired the most famous and respected portrait artist in the city to render in painting their likenesses. When finally these paintings were finished, they were unveiled at a grand evening party. The two hosts themselves led the most influential art connoisseur and critic up to the wall upon which the portraits were hanging side by side. "What do you think?" they asked. The critic studied the portraits for a long time. And then shaking his head, as though there were something that he had missed, he pointed to the space between the portraits and asked, "But where is the savior?"*

Elsa was in a foul mood. Father had come home very late the previous night, and while he slept, Mother had taken the house keys and locked him inside his bedchamber. Had she done this before? Yes, Mother often locked up Father while he slept. In the morning when he woke, he pounded on the door and it was only Frau Frederika's fear of her husband damaging the exquisite cherrywood door that caused her to release him from his jail. Mother started a row with Father. But Father was having none of it. And he left. He left Elsa alone with her mother. And once Father left, Mother turned against Elsa, calling her a liar and accusing her of faking her injury. Mother was furious. Mother pulled Elsa by her dull arm and forced her to her knees calling upon her to pray! Oh, but as Mother bent her head—she let go of Elsa's arm—she let go of Elsa to clasp her hands together in prayer. The moment her mother let go, Elsa ran to the door—

Mother is a fanatic, said Elsa.

What will happen when you return home? the doctor asked.

Elsa said, *I sometimes wonder why it is that others don't see what I see.*

The doctor waited.

She asked him, *Don't you fear them? The Germans?*

What have I to fear? he asked.

He looked at the girl.

In her brown dress and stockings.

A girl—

She held her lame arm.

She twisted her face into a frown.

And then she laughed.

Elsa laughed.

Her laughter turned into a violent fit of coughing.

The doctor waited.

The doctor asked her, *What happened to the child?*

Elsa said, *Two Italian policemen are approached by a lost American traveler. He asks them in English for directions to the Sistine Chapel. They don't understand him, so he tries again in French. No, no, still they do not understand. The traveler tries finally in German, and getting no response, he gives up, scratches his head, and wanders away as lost as when he started out.*

Says one policeman, "I think we should learn a foreign language, don't you? It might be useful."

"*I don't see why,*" says the other. "*That traveler knew several, and it didn't help him.*"

Dr. Apfel, undeterred, repeated his question.

Do you see, he said, *that you cradle your arm like a child?* he asked.

What child? she said.

LESSON 56

She hammered a nail into the wall
Sie hat einen Nagel in die Wand geschlagen

———≈———

Anna set her cup upon its saucer.

The black cat with white boots leapt from the window ledge.

"Maman—Mother—adored Elsa," said Anna.

Eliza asked, "What happened?"

Lemon leaned forward.

Anna said, "I never saw Maman quite so happy as when they sat together at the piano bench. And I knew that it pleased Father that Mother had a friend. Mother was so lonely. But when she was with Elsa, she was happy. Elsa was—"

The brown cat jumped on the table.

"What did she look like?" asked Lemon.

"She was the prettiest girl I had ever seen," said Anna.

The cat nosed the teacups.

"Elsa was Father's great failure. She was his grand disappointment."

Afternoon darkened into evening.

"I always feared—" Anna broke off.

The cat found the cream.

"That Father was in love with her."

"Oh," said Eliza.

"So—" said Lemon.

A clock struck the hour.

"But, of course," said Anna. "I couldn't have been more wrong about that."

She was tired.

She leaned back against her chair.

Could they return again tomorrow?

Anna said, "Father didn't love Elsa. He hated her."

LESSON 57

He has reason to complain, don't you think?
Er hat Grund, sich zu beschweren, glauben Sie nicht?

———

Mrs. Amalie Leopold in a smart wraparound dress of turquoise velour and high side-zippered black boots, carrying her pocketbook matching but exactly her Persian lamb coat, was late for a luncheon date on a sunny afternoon in November 1976.

It could not be helped. Her mother-in-law had called asking if, in her opinion, fowl or fish was a more preferable option for a surprise party she was planning. Mrs. Leopold, the younger, who at that moment sat at her dressing table balancing the telephone against one ear, no hands, while tweezing unnecessarily her eyebrows as she looked into the vanity mirror, asked the elder Mrs. Leopold: *What party?* And by the time the two had confabulated over whether chicken Kiev or dilled salmon was a more appropriately *surprising* entrée, the morning had slipped away. Still, Mrs. Leopold, then barefoot, two, four, eight, ten perfectly perfect toes polished pearly luminous, wearing a satin robe over a nightdress of emerald silk, had not hurried. She undressed; naked before the mirror, she brushed her hair. She applied: eye shadow, mascara, and lipstick. She dressed. She fastened her black lace brassiere; pulled on her nylon stockings. She wrapped herself into her wraparound dress, cinched the belt, zipped up her boots, buttoned her coat, knotted her scarf, picked up her matching pocketbook, and left the house, already a half-hour late.

Mrs. Leopold pulled into the parking lot in a Mercedes sedan of a color best described as *sand.* The car door opened, caught the sun, two legs emerged, the door closed, and all of Mrs. Leopold appeared. She paused for a moment, locked the car door, removed with leather-gloved hands her sunglasses, snapped open her handbag, placed keys and glasses safely inside and walked with no speed or urgency toward the restaurant.

In strode Mrs. Leopold.

She gave a soft, rather elegant sigh at the sight of her luncheon date.

The girl was sitting alone at a table in the corner reading a paper-back novel.

She turned her spoon round and round in her teacup.

The girl looked up from the page.

Amalie did not apologize to the girl, who stood to accept a per-fumed embrace.

Mrs. Leopold removed her coat, ungloved her hands, and set her gloves upon the table.

The girl closed her book.

"Why haven't you ordered yet? asked Mrs. Leopold.

"I was waiting," the girl said.

Mrs. Leopold did not take this as censure for her own lateness, but rather as a sign of her companion's indecision.

"I wish it would snow," the girl said.

Mrs. Leopold looked at the girl's teacup.

"Wouldn't you rather have coffee?" she asked.

The girl nodded.

The waitress arrived and Mrs. Leopold ordered two cups of coffee. She ordered two spinach salads with dressing on the side. Does it come with bread? she asked. She made the waitress repeat the order back to her. The waitress was familiar with the habits of ladies in smart outfits and repeated the order back without a trace of irony.

"Where is the *junkman* today?" asked Mrs. Leopold.

"He's at work," the girl said.

"*Work?*"

"The store," the girl said.

"Why don't you—" began Mrs. Leopold, but she broke off discreetly as the waitress returned with the coffee.

The waitress removed the teacup and saucer.

And Mrs. Leopold finished her sentence: "Come home with me this afternoon? Mitch is out of town—and I have to tell you—"

"What happened," said the girl. "Did he—"

"I can't talk about it *here,*" said Mrs. Leopold.

A lady at a nearby table waved to Mrs. Leopold, a tiny gesture with fork held aloft between her fingers.

The girl lowered her voice.

Her blonde hair was long and straight.

Her eyes were blue.

She bit her lip.

"Tell me, Amy," she whispered. "Are you going to run away with him?"

Mrs. Leopold did not answer.

Mrs. Leopold looked particularly complete today.

Her face was *beautiful.* Her car: *sand.* Her hair: *diamond.* Her dress: *turquoise.*

She turned her wedding ring round and round her finger.

The waitress brought the two salads with dressing on the side, and a basket of French bread. Mrs. Leopold studied the order in search of flaws, but finding none, she unfolded her napkin and placed it on her lap.

The girl said, "Sometimes I miss Hedy so much. Sometimes I imagine that she's a ghost—you know, right here with us. Is that strange? Do you ever—"

Mrs. Leopold delved with her fork into the heap of dark leafy spinach.

The girl buttered her bread.

Mrs. Leopold looked at the girl.

"You really should do something about your hair," she said.

She picked up the paperback that the girl had left on the table.

"Don't you ever get tired of romance novels?" she asked.

"What's wrong with romance?" asked the girl.

"I'm tired of romance," said Mrs. Leopold.

She handed the book back to the girl.

"I'm pregnant," Mrs. Leopold said.

Said the girl, "Oh Amy, I'm so happy—"

"Are you?" said Mrs. Leopold. "Are you really?"

"You're so lucky," said the girl.

"Shut up," said Mrs. Leopold. "Please just shut up, will you?"

The waitress cleared away the plates.

She asked if the ladies would like dessert today?

The girl turned toward the window. She rubbed her eyes.

"Is the sun bothering you?" asked the waitress. "Would you like me to lower the blinds?"

The girl shook her head.

She looked as though she might cry.

Mrs. Leopold knew what was best for the girl, and she certainly didn't want her to start crying right there in the middle of the crowded restaurant.

"Do you have strawberry shortcake?" Mrs. Leopold asked the waitress.

And the waitress said, "Yes, baked fresh this morning."

Mrs. Leopold touched the girl on the arm. The girl wiped her eyes with her napkin.

"Do you have whipped cream?" Mrs. Leopold asked.

"My sister will have the strawberry shortcake with whipped cream," Mrs. Leopold told the waitress.

Petra couldn't stop crying, and she buried her face in her arm.

LESSON 58

Please place a saucer under the cup
Stellen sie bitte einen Teller unter die Tasse

⁓

What about the baby?

Lemon Leopold, she of stage and screen, the big laugh, the dramatic pause, the drum roll, the pratfall and pout, the close-up, the white skin, the wide eyes, the fair hair; the exquisite ingénue did not know that her father was Louis Apollinaire, the zookeeper, with whom Mrs. Mitchell Leopold had kept time during the summer and then into the autumn of 1976, but he was gone—into the wild—that winter.

And before her?

Eliza: born to Hedy and Samuel Berlin. Hedy Apfel eloped with Samuel Berlin. Hedy wanted to run away. She wanted to escape her—*ghosts*. They rented a cabin on a lake. The summer season over; the vacationers gone. Dark water crashed upon the shore. And they sat on the shore and watched the dark water. It was windy. It grew cold. Someone called her name. *Hedy!* She looked. She saw. She saw wandering the shore: men with pant legs rolled, children digging for shells. The ladies were taking care not to let the hems of their dresses drag in the water. Hedy grabbed Sam's hand and pulled him up. And Hedy and Sam took off running down the beach. Where did they go? Where was there to go? They ran. *Let's go. Let's go.*

And then?

Hedy died. And no one liked to talk too much about what had happened to Hedy. She died, and Petra came to take care of the baby. Petra was nineteen. Petra loved Sam. And Amalie hated him: the junkman. Sam sat in his store and read books. Sam gave Petra books. And she read them. While towels tumbled in the dryer. While the just-washed floor dried pine-bright. Sam gave Petra instruction in the classics. But she had a taste for sweeter fiction. She worked at Wollstonecraft, but she flew through *The Thorn Birds*. And *Princess Daisy*. She needed Norah Lofts. She ravaged Belva Plain. She loved Howard Fast. Slim paperbacks quickened her pulse. Hefty tomes were exquisite torture. Late at night her footsteps creaked on the wooden floorboards of their falling-down house. She studied. On sunny mornings in the garden among her lilacs and lilies. In the kitchen as dough rose. And Petra learned. And all that Petra learned about love she taught to Eliza.

What about the baby before that?

To Mitch and Amy came Benjamin Leopold—doted upon by his father, raised to question; to be de- and inductive; to ask; to listen; to probe; to be abstract and concrete; to theorize; hypothesize; to analyze—he remembered his childhood. And as such he could not escape hating his mother.

What train traveled all along the Apfel line?

One, two, three—Amalie, Hedy, and Petra—little *Mädchen* were born to Margot Apfel, the second frau of Herr Franz.

And before that?

A baby was left one night in a basket on the steps of a temple. How like Moses in the reeds—a prince of Egypt! The rabbi found the basket. He pondered the situation. No one came forward to claim the child; it was the Rabbi Berlin who called the boy Samuel and raised him.

Before that?

Diminutive Dot nearly died of it, and she told all who cared to listen and many who did not care to about the grueling days-long labor from which was delivered forth the very large-headed and round-bellied miracle that was to be Mitchell Leopold.

No, no! Go back further!

Elsa tried to get rid of hers. She took spoonfuls of castor oil and laxatives. Magda said try quinine and pennyroyal; gin, slippery elm bark, and hot mustard baths. Elsa said she would use a coat hanger or knitting needle or *Füllerhalter!* And as each remedy failed, the girl grew frantic. She would throw herself from a bridge or take poison. Magda said it wasn't as bad as all that; that Elsa needn't be so dramatic. But Elsa cried that she had seen in a dream—the future!—What would happen?—A horrible death—unspeakable—for this child. How could she bear such suffering? Better not to begin than to suffer such a terrible end! *Will you help me?* Elsa asked Magda. *Oh darling!* cried Magda. *When have I done anything but? Haven't I given you all that I have? Even my husband I gave to you!* Frau Magda Kaufmann took Elsa to a doctor. *You are lucky to know me,* said Magda. *To have me.* She had found a doctor, and not some filthy-handed hack; he used anesthetic—he kept a back room for nice girls in trouble, that is, girls who could pay—and Elsa needn't worry. On the way to the office, Elsa saw a man kick a barking dog in the street. And a lady stuck her head out of an upper window and shouted at the man. He shouted back. Magda took Elsa's hand and hurried her along.

And after that?

Hart Luther railed about oceans, oil, and opium fields; about the slave trade; jokes and their relation to the unconscious; about hostages and captors. Why did Hart and Eliza marry? Was there a child? Yes—of course—because of the baby; because Eliza was pregnant. Because even if love is terrorism, terrorism has its obligations. And Hart and Eliza went to Berlin.

LESSON 59

Grimms' fairy tales are very popular with children
Grimms Märchen sind bei Kindern sehr beliebt

━━━━

Tulla told Dolfi that she saw Franz kissing Elsa in the garden.

LESSON 60

Can we change the subject?
Können wir das Thema wechseln?

———

Doctor Apfel asked Elsa to tell him about the operation.

She said, *I lay flat upon the table.*

Elsa lay flat on the table.

Silver instruments were set upon a tray.

Magda held Elsa's hand. They awaited the doctor.

Elsa broke from her memory to clarify, *Not you, Sir, a different doctor. A different doctor altogether though the same patient.*

He came in. He gave his patient ether.

He disappeared again.

Elsa said to Magda, *Have you ever wondered how it is that cats have two holes cut into their skin precisely at the place where their eyes are?*

Magda shushed her.

Magda laid a cool plump hand upon Elsa's forehead.

Magda said that she was not supposed to tell because it was a secret but Herr Kaufmann had bought Elsa a pretty locket, and a pearl ring, too, for her troubles. Otto did so adore her.

The doctor came back.

Still awake? he asked.

Doctor, Doctor, she said.

He gave his patient more medicine.

Elsa breathed deep of the ether.

She closed her eyes.

She slept.

She dreamed.

She woke.

Elsa told Dr. Apfel that when she awoke, she was in Frau Kaufmann's bed.

Dr. Apfel asked Elsa why it was that she told jokes.

Elsa sighed.

These very serious jokes, she said.

Elsa was nineteen in 1919.

She asked the doctor, *Am I symbolic of the century?*

She asked him a riddle.

What is it—she said—*that is greater than the universe; the dead cannot eat; and if the living do, they will die?*

She sat upon the sofa.

In Dr. Apfel's office among the sphinx statuettes—

There were no clocks.

Time is tricky. Or so it seemed to Elsa.

Shall I tell you the answer? she asked.

She leaned back against the cushions of the sofa.

LESSON 61

Are you jealous of your son's wife?
Sind Sie eifersüchtig auf die Frau Ihres Sohnes?

———

What about Elsa?

Doctor Apfel tried the key in the lock.

He worked through Elsa's case. It had happened as such:

Herr K. grabbed Elsa's arm during their first tryst.

Elsa slapped Herr K. She could no longer feel her arm or move the fingers of this very hand. Her arm had become symbolic of her secret, her child. She continued—to collect—the loss as part of her body. She cradled her arm like a child. Elsa's paranoia could be traced to her loss and her loss to her guilt and her guilt to her desire and her desire to her guilt and her guilt to her loss; until, overwhelmed, the girl projected her guilt upon the faces of strangers, ordinary Germans, in the street.

The key—stuck—would not turn quite as the doctor desired.

Was it a tremor in his hand? Or a fault of the mechanism?

Something drew him—with anticipation always for his next hour with her—to his young patient. What was so elusive about Elsa?

Was it her hysteria?

Was it her fanatical mother or her libidinous father?

Was it her story of deceit, desire, and seduction?

Her affair with Herr Otto K. Or her operation?

Was it her obsession? Or her paranoia? Her dreams?

The doctor saw in Elsa's dreams only familiar symbols.

She was no prognosticator; no more a bearer of premonitions than any other neurotic girl. The doctor neither believed nor disbelieved her visions; such a judgment would have been irrelevant to her treatment. What drew the doctor to Elsa?

The doctor sat at his desk.

Elsa had just left him.

Her absence in his office was palpable.

He set pen to paper.

He reasoned. He wrote—

No words came to him.

In the kitchen Dolfi stirred a pot of pudding.

In the master's *Schlafzimmer*, Tulla sang as she changed the bedsheets.

Anna in the nursery pondered the wooden pieces of a jigsaw puzzle.

Franz fell asleep over his studies.

Upstairs Madame Madeline played long-fingered an étude.

And then the doctor knew; he knew.

It was not Elsa who so interested him. It had never been—

It was not really *Elsa* at all.

The catch—caught—the key turned so smoothly—

It was Madame Madeline.

LESSON 62

Allow tablet to dissolve in mouth
Im Mund zergehen lassen

———————

The doctor loved his young bride.

Yet she, as the years passed, his talented and lovely wife, remained and grew more so, unfathomable, unreadable, unreachable, marble-solid, impenetrable, uninterpretable to him.

And he sought through his patient Elsa—his wife's friend and dear chosen companion—to find—to see, to touch, to investigate, to hold in his hand, to dissect, to walk through the many chambers of—the mysterious heart of Madame Madeline.

The doctor adored Madeline.

He loved her delicacy and elegance.

He confessed his love—nightly—to her.

He kept secret another trait he cherished in his wife.

Madame Madeline had no sense of humor.

Dr. Apfel found a sense of humor in a woman to be vulgar and extraneous—vestigial, even—like a tail. If it had once served a purpose, it no longer had use; and now was an ugly remnant of a less civilized age. To hear a woman tell a joke was like watching a monkey play a cardboard violin at the circus. It was an imitation of comedy. And the doctor had reason to ruminate upon the topic of jokes; for ever since his encounter with Udo, the young joke-telling soldier, Dr. Apfel had been compiling his own analytical epic, his *Jokework*.

The joke—jests; jibes; bawdy, blasphemous, infantile, erotic; tricks of wordplay; puns and double entendres; gags; games; gaffs—jokes—had become his life's work.

Udo had used jokes for the purpose of seducing girls. It was upon the foundation of Udo's case that the doctor built his triangular seduction theory.

The first premise of the theory was simply: a joke involves a teller, the person told, and the person upon whom the burden of the joke falls.

Call them: *the seducer, the seduced,* and *the desired object.*

And while the doctor saw the necessity of the woman (or the *desired object)* in the circuitry of the joke, he did not in his *Jokework* discuss jokes told by women. He found nothing *interesting* or *illuminating* about the idea or expression of humor in women. And so it followed—logically—that he had no interest in those jokes that they might tell. No, no: he believed truly that humor, like vulgarity and violence, was beneath a civilized woman. And the presence of dear humorless Madame Madeline, who talked of politics and played the piano and wrote letters in the garden, proved correct at least this much of his theory.

Elsa's jokes infuriated the doctor.

How could he explain Elsa and her jokes?

She laughed without laughing.

Elsa's jokes were symptomatic—or perhaps illustrative—of her hostile seductive exhibitionism. But who was the third leg of the joker's triangle?

LESSON 63

Where does Rome lie? Rome lies on the Tiber
Wo liegt Rom? Rom liegt am Tiber

———

Dolfi didn't tell anyone save Tulla how once when she was bringing cakes warm from the oven to the ladies in the parlor, she saw Madame in dark silk and her student in a smart brown frock sitting together at the piano bench. Madame Madeline had one hand upon the nape of the girl's neck, and with the other she caressed Elsa's hair. Elsa with her head resting on Madeline's shoulder twined her fingers in the knotted strands of Madame's pearl necklace.

The doctor's wife held Elsa's face in her white white hands—

Oh! Madame's eyes for a moment rested right upon Dolfi in the doorway.

And Madame Madeline kissed Elsa.

Dolfi turned away—down the hall—and though she wanted to run—she couldn't—she didn't—for she worried that she might upset her tray of cream cakes and tea.

LESSON 64

Tie a knot in your handkerchief to remind you
Mach die einen Knoten ins Taschentuch, damit du's nicht vergisst

———

In February of 1925, a team of sled dogs led by a valiant Siberian husky, Balto, raced to finish a 650-mile trek with medicine to save the diphtheria-devastated citizens of snowed-in Nome, Alaska. The story captured the public imagination. Wolf Luther was in California when he read about it in the papers. What was he doing? Rubbing tanning oil on Norma Shearer's shoulders? Sitting on a stool in Schwab's drinking a chocolate soda? Working the squares of a crossword puzzle? Hitler's *Mein Kampf* was published in Germany the same year. Where was Franz Apfel? Strolling along the Seine in Paris with his bride? Balto only led the last leg of the journey, but who could begrudge him the glory? And that April, when a German serial killer, Fritz Haarmann, *the butcher of Hanover*, who murdered twenty-six boys and sold their flesh as meat, was executed by decapitation; where was Dr. Apfel? In his quiet study ruminating on the great sleight of hand that led the apes to the apples? Was he troubled by the fact that he did not— could not—cure Elsa Z.? And as he turned the pages of his appointment book, looking at tomorrow and the day after, did he fear and hope and wonder for the future?

In 1927 Lindbergh flew solo across the Atlantic.

In 1928 Alexander Fleming discovered penicillin.

In 1930—Anna at fifteen years old—as curious as any girl in a house full of secrets—one afternoon when Father was out lecturing to university students on the topic of *Alas, Poor Yorick: The Psychopathology of Forgetfulness*—walked down the long hallway to his office; entered the sunny outer room; turned the key in the lock; turned the knob of the second door; passed into that inner office, and searched through her father's files until she found the document for which she had come: *The Case of Elsa Z.*

She sat at her father's desk.

And she read. And she learned.

Father had written page after page.

About Elsa's dreams.

About Elsa's fears.

The windows were open.

A warm fall wind came in—

And blew the pages—

Anna learned that a dream contained symbols.

And that a symbol replaced what was real.

Elsa dreamed of destruction.

Elsa thought that the German people wanted to kill her.

Why did Elsa think that the Germans wanted to kill her?

Father knew that hysterical neurotics locked up their pain in a jewel box and kept it safe and guarded it against harm. Father knew that when a problem was imaginary, the solution to that problem would be a terrible thing.

Anna looked about Father's room where secrets were confessed.

What a pleasant room—with its vases and marble gods.

With the paintings—of Oedipus and the Sphinx; of the capture of Joseph; the seduction of Leda; the Madonna and child; of Moses on the Nile.

With the framed alpine postcards: scenes from dear little German towns that so charmed Father—the church spires, a carnival, the rivers, the mountains, the forests.

With the lingering smoke of Father's tobacco.

The threadbare roses of the Persian rug.

And the sofa, which bore the imprint of some ghost body.

Anna read until there were no more pages to read.

Father came to no conclusion about whether there was hope for Elsa.

For Father's analysis ended abruptly.

Upon the typewritten page—a note—in Father's cryptic script—

Like the doves in the plum trees—the proof of a dream may rest in its very improbability. For what one dreams is always possible. And this is the worst truth of all.

She stood at the window and looked out at the garden.

She remembered Elsa.

There was no need for Father to believe Elsa.

He hated that he could not heal her.

Dr. Apfel hated Elsa.

He loved Germany.

There is nothing that is funny that is not in some way horrible.

And worse: there is nothing horrible that is not in some way funny.

There was no conclusion to *The Case of Elsa Z.*

Anna filed the papers away back where she had found them.

Anna left her father's office that afternoon. And she grew up.

Berlin was sinking into the dark waters of the Spree.

Frankenstein's monster rose from the table.

Leave Berlin—Father's students said. Let's go, let's go. They said that it was time to go—

No more raucous six-day bicycle races; no more Wernher von Braun and the *Society for Space Travel* angling rockets at the moon. No more Lotte Lenya. No more Erich Maria Remarque; he spent his nights in New York at 21 and The Stork Club pitching screenplays and wooing starlets. No more Josephine Baker dancing naked in her *Chocolate Kiddies Revue* upon the stage at the Wintergarten. Leni

Riefenstahl, the rucksack-toting sylph of wholesome mountain movies, took up a motion picture camera and glorified the manly arts of tug-of-war and communal bathing. *The Cabinet of Dr. Caligari* was closed—or permanently pried open.

Berlin, the metropolis, tipped and tottered between sadism and masochism.

In carnival booths clairvoyants asked: *What happens next?*

Fortunetellers, phrenologists, table-turners, tarot-card readers, magicians, and mesmerists predicted mayhem. Erik Jan Hanussen, the occult impresario and *psychic detective,* who foretold both Hitler's rise and fall based on his horoscope, was shot dead in the street.

In 1932 James Chadwick discovered the neutron.

In 1933 Hitler gained power.

In 1935 the Nuremberg laws passed.

Jews were stripped of German citizenship.

In 1936 the Spanish Civil War; the BBC ran its first televised transmission; and the Olympic Games were held in Berlin.

The stadium was festooned with advertisements for Coca-Cola.

In 1937 Anna left Berlin. She was twenty-two. Father secured her passage on a ship to England. She left from Hamburg. What a day it had been. Father was ill. He walked with a cane. Mother's dark dress seemed shabby in the sunlight.

Mother gave Anna her pearls.

Anna disembarked in Southampton.

Dr. Apfel would not leave Berlin.

Madame Madeline would not leave her husband.

In 1938 Nestlé introduced instant coffee.

The Nazis annexed Austria.

Anna read it about in a newspaper.

Names and places and people began to disappear.

There were no more picture postcards from father.

With dogs or castles or alpine scenes upon them.

The window of Aron's butcher shop was smashed in.

The floor was covered with bits of broken glass.

Tulla and Dolfi were put on a train. Later Elsa's family too: her sisters; her mother and father. And Frau Magda and Herr Otto Kaufmann; the girls Käthe and Greta.

Doctor Apfel never left Berlin.

On a day in November, Dr. Apfel gave to his wife a dose of morphine.

Madame Madeline lay in her black dress across the bed.

And then the doctor took his own medicine.

1939 nylon stockings were invented. And the Second World War broke out.

LESSON 65

Somebody really ought to tell her
Man müsste es ihr eigentlich sagen

───

What did Elsa dream?

We are traveling on a train at night in the dark. Not we, but I. I am in a dark compartment. The train stops. I get off at an unfamiliar station. It is snowing. I see Father and Theodor walking ahead along a road into a town. I call after them, but they do not hear me. I follow them, but I cannot seem to catch up. They are so far away. No matter how fast I follow, they do not get closer. I stumble over an open suitcase lying in the snow. It is full of gold coins. There are so many that I cannot count them. I can no longer see Father or Theodor; where have they gone? When I look down again, the suitcase is not full of coins but gold teeth. Where are Father and Theodor? I drag the suitcase; it is so heavy. I drag the suitcase through the snow and keep walking even though it is dark and cold and I don't know where I am going.

LESSON 66

I would also like to buy a few picture postcards of Vienna
Ich möchte auch einige Ansichtskarten von Wien kaufen

What is the problem with psychoanalysis?

Dr. Benjamin Leopold, when he was eleven years old and called Benjy, spent New Year's Eve 1976—with his grandfather. While his parents had gone to a party. And Franz and Benjy stayed up late and watched television; they saw the shimmering ball drop in Times Square. Franz opened the cages and let his parakeets and lovebirds fly around the house. Benjy slept that night in his mother's old bedroom. And he remembered waking in the darkness to the sound of voices; he went downstairs and there at the kitchen table sat Grandfather drinking tea and eating cake with a girl in an old-fashioned dress. A green bird sat perched on Grandfather's shoulder. Ben recalled how before she took a sip, the girl turned her spoon round and round in the china cup.

Benjy watched his grandfather and the girl.

And even years later he did not divulge this memory to his therapist, to Dr. de Groot.

What it meant—the memory—he did not want to understand.

What did it mean?

This was Ben's first ghost.

Ben saw the ghost of his grandfather's first wife; the girl called Charlotte Blau.

LESSON 67

His dog even offers his paw to shake hands
Sein Hund gibt sogar die Pfote

———————

Doesn't that just take the cake?

The antique shop was called without embellishment or apostrophe: Berlin.

There were curiosities and curios: postcards; sofas and chairs; figurines and photographs. There were clocks of various manner and variety: grandfather, cuckoo, travel, metal, wood, tin, tiny, broken, loud, charming, chiming, alarming, novelty, necessary, familiar, and foreign.

And all the clocks rang the wrong time.

It had seemed to each of them in succession, Ben, Eliza, and Lemon, when they were children, that there must be one clock somewhere in the shop that told the right time; and that if this clock could be found—a great mystery would be revealed.

What was the mystery?

Eliza's father locked the door at night.

In the morning he unlocked the door.

There were many rooms—a labyrinth—

Victorian valentines, lunchboxes with the faces of forgotten television stars.

There was no regard to order or sequence.

It was easy to get lost.

Isn't it easy to get lost?

Berlin was heaped high and low with silverware, comic books, brass doorknobs, bolts of faded fabric, soda bottles, bicycles, baubles, baby dolls with painted faces, bracelets, bric-a-brac, Persian rugs, portraits of parrots and paintings of ships lost at sea, salt shakers, sugar bowls, tuneless radios, model trains and miniature stations, suitcases, shoes, coats, clocks, wristwatches, rings, sewing machines, mementos, mirrors, postcards of happier times and times not so happy, photographs and cameras, cups, copper, coins, and candlesticks. There were perverse gnomes, grinning Hansels and handsome Gretels, milk-glass swans, painted seashells, broken hearts and bone china, candy boxes long emptied of sweetness, metronomes, tureens and tablecloths, plates commemorating the World's Fair and the accomplishments of astronauts, spoons dulled from an eternity of dipping, dogs who danced and madcap monkeys who clapped cymbals at the winding of a key.

History was heaped up on the shelves of the shop; it was gimcrack-corny; page-frayed, rabbit-eared, ringding, riddle-thick, and cast-off-ghost crowded.

Ben saw ghosts.

Eliza wanted to see ghosts.

And Lemon didn't need to *see* to *believe* in them.

When they were children—

There was a place called Berlin.

And Berlin was a place that existed outside of time.

LESSON 68

They say that industry is going to make increasing use of robots
In der Industrie sollen mehr Roboter eingesetzt werden

⎯⎯⎯

Lemon was watching television in her hotel room.
 It was a movie about a haunted house.
 The telephone rang.
 It was Ben.
 He asked her if she was going to take the role of Gretchen in
Faust?
 She asked him what time it was back home?
 They talked about politics and war.
 They talked about the deep roots of trees.
 About angels and devils and deals.
 Lemon's hair was violet.
 Her nails were lacquered black.
 They talked as a brother and sister will.
 They spoke of Mother and Father.
 They talked of luck and lack and baseball.
 They talked about civilization and its discontents.
 And the difference between dreams and stories.
 And how a dream is real—
 At least to its dreamer—
 More real than a joke.
 Or an ink pen or a bar of soap.

More real than history.

Even better than historical: *factual*.

More factual than a bat or ball or brick.

Ben believed that their family was unlike other families.

Ben wanted to know why Anna was telling her story *now*.

Lemon said, wouldn't he rather just hear the story?

She tried to tell him about Anna and about Elsa.

He interrupted her.

She forgave him.

Because she knew him, after all.

He didn't want to hear Anna's story.

He said he had listened to too many ghost stories.

He said his patients were obligated to their own nightmares.

What is more absurd than an obligation to the unreal?

He was an expert at the identification of problems.

And after a problem is identified, it can be solved.

Ben spoke of epistemology.

And how we know what we know.

He spoke of science and the soul.

He spoke of genetics—

Of blood.

Of the brain, of neural pathways and neurotic behaviors.

He spoke of God.

And chemicals.

And *chance* and *destiny*.

Of the *inevitable* and the *impossible*.

Ben had always believed that he could help—he could cure—his patients. But what if he couldn't? Was he destined to fail them? His patients clung to their problems. How could he help if they would not let go of their pain? Just as his patients clung to their pain—

Did he hold onto his failure out of a fear of something worse?

Lemon listened.

She said, wasn't there a wonderful mystery to things?

Ben said, "What mystery?"

Ben said, "What things?"

He said that a train simply follows the track.

If it strays from the track—disaster—

Ben did not want to believe that Anna was the real Anna Apfel, because the fact of her existence changed the plot of stories upon which he relied to keep himself on track.

What is more intentional than an accident?

Lemon said that she wasn't talking about trains or tracks, but about mystery.

On television—

In the movie: a girl in a white nightdress was trying to get out of the house.

The doors were locked.

Ben said that he had never really loved Betts.

He loved the idea of her.

And then he grew to hate the idea of her.

And after hate came fear.

Or maybe the fear had come first.

He had never hated her.

Only *the idea* of her.

It was hard to know the order of things.

It was hard to know a thing.

Ben was lost.

So he picked a spot, a place—by the swimming pool.

And he waited.

One must *know,* rather than *feel.*

One must *be,* rather than *seem.*

And what is more accidental than intention?

He asked her if she knew the story of the Wandering Jew?

Ben told her the story of the Wandering Jew.

A legend arose about a shoemaker who taunted Jesus on his way to crucifixion. And that this shoemaker said to Jesus: *Go on quicker.*

And that as punishment this shoemaker was said to walk the earth—to wander from place to place—until the second coming.

The character had many names: in German, *Der Ewige Jude;* in French, *Le Juif Errant* and *L'Ebreo Errante;* and in Spanish, *Juan Espera en Dios.*

There were sightings of this eternal Jew—

An Albanian monk swore a Jew called Ahasuerus dined with him at his table. A portrait painter in Amsterdam said a dark-winged Jew flew into his rooms at midnight, bringing with him the element of fire. An alchemist in Hamburg said he saw a Jew called Josef in ragged clothing, and barefoot, walking through a storm of ice.

Lemon on the bed leaned back against the pillows.

The girl began to climb the winding staircase.

The girl in the white nightdress was so beautiful.

The girl fell.

The girl had fallen.

Ben talked about terror and pity.

Ben said: "Jew."

Ben kept saying: "Jew."

Was it funny?

Wasn't it funny?

Not just a little bit?

It was funny but terrible too.

Ben spoke the word as though he had only just learned it.

The girl's dress was torn.

And exactly but exactly one bare breast was revealed.

Was it funny?

How funny was it?

Ben said that he had read Martin Luther's *On the Jews and Their Lies.*

He had found it on her bookshelf, he said.

She said that anything was possible.

Ben said, "Listen to this: 'If we wish to wash our hands of the Jews' blasphemy and not share in their guilt, we have to part company with them. They must be driven from our country.—Set fire to their synagogues or schools and to bury and cover with dirt whatever will not burn, so that no man will ever again see a stone or cinder of them. This is to be done in honor of our Lord and of Christendom, so that God might see that we are Christians.'"

Lemon burst out laughing.

Why are terrible things so funny?

Lemon felt just then that she was a Jew in Berlin.

Why had it not occurred to her until that moment that she was a Jew in Berlin?

Ben asked her, "Isn't it strange? To be there?"

"Do you feel strange?" Ben asked Lemon.

"I never feel strange," said Lemon. "I always feel that I am just where I should be."

Le Juif Errant!

Ben spoke of Germany at night.

A figure in black approached the girl.

The girl was clutching the torn fabric of her nightdress.

There was a knock on Lemon's door.

Room service arrived with her dinner.

With boiled beef and sour bread.

With *Stroh und Lehm*. And salty *Shrapnellsuppe*.

Oh, for dessert there was warm chocolate cake with cherries.

What a revelation!

LESSON 69

The floor is covered with pieces of broken glass
Auf dem Boden liegen lauter Scherben

———————

Mrs. Amalie Leopold, wearing an exquisite white gown tied over one shoulder in the Athenian goddess style, which flattered her bronzed bare skin—as well as disguising her slightly rounded belly—sat at a table with her dear friends Mrs. Eloise Schiff and Mrs. Betsy Green, and their respective husbands, Paul and Bernie.

Their staid country club had been transformed into a tropical paradise for the party. An irreverent artist of *trompe l'oeil* stylings had painted scrolling murals on paper, which now hung, unfurled, over the walls of the dining room.

The effect was magical: a green rain forest shimmered and surrounded the drunken celebrants of New Year's Eve 1976.

Flowers flowered, birds flew, fish swam in pristine pools of blue, and tigers lounged with great resolve. The waitresses wore leopard-print leotards. The busboys: dun safari outfits with pith helmets. And if the string quartet, attired in indefatigable black was oddly incongruous with the tropical theme, no one minded; no one noticed.

Dr. Mitchell Leopold, standing at the bar, was struck suddenly by the idea of his own good fortune. He had always been lucky. He had never looked for luck, but he had never been ungrateful or indulgent when it had found him. He looked across the room at Amy, his beautiful wife.

He turned to the man seated beside him.

"So which one is yours?" Mitch asked.

The man looked up from his drink.

"Excuse me?" he said.

"Which one," repeated the doctor. "Who are you here with?"

"I'm not," the man said.

The man drank.

"Do you believe in luck?" asked Mitch.

The man said that he supposed that he *did* believe in luck.

Without another word he picked up his glass and walked away, but his exit was slowed by a limp, by the dragging of his left foot by his right. Dr. Leopold watched him go. And Louis Apollinaire, when he left the dining room to the string quartet's strains, walked directly and not unintentionally past the table of Mrs. Leopold.

Amy—only moments later—rose from her chair.

Eloise was reassuring her husband about the professionalism of their teenaged babysitter. And Betsy toughed it out with an overdone cut of prime rib.

Mrs. Leopold, in white, left the dining room.

Amalie walked past the powder room, turned a corner; she looked down one hallway and then the next. She made her way to the club library. She paused to remove her high-heeled shoes; picked them up; carrying them, she continued on, barefoot down the dimly lighted corridor.

Amy Leopold turned the doorknob, stepped into the room—

He sat awaiting her in the otherwise dark room, surrounded by a semicircle of light cast by the green-domed table lamp. Palms idled in beau-pots and on pedestals ivy tangled.

The draperies were closed; the outside world shut out.

Amy stood in the doorway.

Her white dress was—just briefly—transparent.

"Sit," he said. "Please."

She pulled the door shut and joined him in the library.

She set her shoes on the plush plum carpet.

She sat on the leather sofa.

"I read somewhere," she said, "that when you are lost in the woods, you should stay in one place and wait."

"Have you ever been lost in the woods?" he asked.

She curled her legs beneath her.

Her nails, finger and toe, were painted silver.

"I can imagine," she said.

There was a glass beside him on the table.

He did not drink from it.

She asked him why he was here.

"Here?" he said.

"Don't get existential on me," she said. "I only want to know why you are at this party—"

He said that he knew that she was going to be here.

And that he had to tell her—

He said that he was leaving soon.

"Yes," she said. "It's a rotten party."

That wasn't what he meant.

She knew what he meant, but ignored it.

"Isn't it rotten?" she said. "Isn't this just the worst?"

He said that he had been in worse places.

"I wouldn't go that far," she said.

"How far would you go?" he asked.

He lighted a cigarette.

He smoked on in the darkness.

She leaned her head back and closed her eyes.

193

A clock ticked.

He said, "You could come with me."

She didn't open her eyes.

Back in the banquet hall a drunken Betsy pushed her dish of mango ice cream across the table to Eloise. Paul told Bernie about his new car, while Mitch glanced at his wristwatch.

Amy did not move.

She sat with her feet curled beneath her on the sofa.

A telephone rang.

She looked around.

There was a telephone on the table beside him.

"Please don't—" she said.

He didn't answer the telephone.

It continued to ring.

It sounded like an alarm clock.

He said, "Have you heard the one about the man who threw his alarm clock out the window? He wanted to see time fly."

Amy Leopold, who knew that his joke wasn't funny, burst out laughing.

LESSON 70

Monkeys, elephants, and lions are wild animals
Affen, Elefanten, und Löwen sind wilde Tiere

⁓

What have you seen so far in Germany?
The shore is crowded with tourists in summer.
In the winter they hit the ski slopes.
Ah, hike the snow-capped mountains—
Sleep under the stars.
The woods, dark and mysterious, await exploration.
Read the tales of E. T. A. Hoffmann.
Read Rilke's elegies.
Mull Mann.
Ponder the films of Fassbinder.
Visit the Berlin Philharmonic.
Listen to Beethoven, Schubert, Schumann, and Mahler.
When you hear the works of Wagner, does your soul not stir?
Ride with the Valkyrie!
Be a falcon, or a storm, or a great song.
See the city at night.
See Berlin: the dance clubs, the beer halls, the cafés and restaurants.
Gamble at the Spielbank Berlin. Go to the Casino Royale.
Play roulette, blackjack, and baccarat at the gaming tables.
Pick a card.
Spin the wheel—

Try your luck.

Your holiday will soon end.

Hurry, hurry! See and savor delicious Berlin, salty and sweet, before God gets hungry and with an outstretched hand and fist and mighty arm grabs it up and gobbles it down dabbed with sour cream and spicy mustard.

Make the most of your remaining time.

Be; do; act.

Change. Grow. Learn. Adapt. Experience. Evolve.

The world is miraculous.

If evolution isn't a miracle, then what is?

No one in the dance clubs, the sex shops, no one eating *Schweinefleisch* in a café; no one zipping up a leather jacket; none of the children with fingers pressed against the aquarium glass knows exactly who killed whom and why.

Your holiday is soon ending.

Do not be downhearted.

This is the future.

Adaptation is a wonder like the great pyramids of Egypt or Babylon's hanging gardens. Possibility is improbable: like winning at roulette or surviving a car crash. Memory expands. And rubber is elastic. Set spoon to saucer.

The trick of time is a disappearing act.

Read your map; follow the route markers.

This way to the future!

You have the whole of the city and all of its delights set out before you—

You must go forward.

What will you see and do today? What will you do next?

LESSON 71

I quickly got used to my new surroundings
Ich habe mich schnell an die neue Umgebung gewöhnt

⎯⎯⎯

In 1938 an industrious German farmer planted russet-colored larch saplings in a pine forest. The trees grew. They thrived in sun and rain and snow and shadow. Year by year they thickened and bloomed and spread. And so it was that for a few weeks each autumn as the leaves turned, travelers arriving to and departing from Berlin's airport, should they look out a window at the rich expanse of countryside, might note the giant shape—could it be? Made by the red leaves against the forest's greener green. And it so happened that when Hart and Eliza looked out the window as they arrived in Berlin on an early November morning in 1990, they saw too what that farmer had had in mind. Hart rang the bell for the stewardess. He wanted to ask her about the swastika growing in the forest. He pointed out the window. He asked in English, but she shook her head. Hart spoke to her in German, but the stewardess did not answer. He tried again in French. She did not understand. And she smiled as she poured out two little cups of coffee—with packets of sugar and cream and plastic spoons—for the travelers.

Hart said, *Danke*.

Eliza said, *Thank you*.

You're welcome, said the stewardess.

LESSON 72

They ran toward the forest
Sie liefen dem Walde zu

———

How good was Eliza's memory?

Hart and Eliza married in a slapdash crazy fit of obligation.

And they went—on what might, in less fanatical company, be called a honeymoon—to Berlin. Hart chose the destination. And although they wandered; they lingered; roamed; meandered; and made their way through streets, gates, promenades, parks, and landmarks, Hart did not find the thing for which he searched. What did he want? His questions went unanswered. He grew irritable; and then lethargic. He didn't like the hotel. He could not get used to the time change. The food was wretched; the weather oppressive; the monuments too monumental. What was his problem?

They saw such things!

An army of environmental protestors—in skull masks and skeleton suits—riding green bicycles took to the streets, stopping traffic; this: the sight of his comrades-in-arms forcing BMWs and Volkswagens to a halt, did not cheer Hart. It sank him deeper into despair. There were too many statues in Berlin. He did not find contrition or apology or explanation. Only a gunmetal-gray, stone, and skyscraper-sharp Erector Set of a city; now, now, now: into the future. Only people going about their lives.

He was twenty-three and she was twenty-one.

She was pregnant.

He hated Germany.

He hated Berlin.

But she loved it.

Her feeling for Germany terrified her.

One afternoon as they sat at a café, Eliza reading an English newspaper and Hart studying train schedules, he said that if they hurried they could catch the S-Bahn to Sachsenhausen. Hart said, *Let's go*. They did not finish their coffee. They ran. They took off running. A light rain fell and was falling as they ran to the train station. He was ahead of her. Berlin was laid out before them; and they ran. He made it to the platform first. And he cried out to her: *Run*, he said, *run*.

To any young bride who has felt sad or uncertain, to those grooms who have thought themselves awkward and unlovable: consider the image of Hart Luther, standing on the platform waiting to be chuffed off to a concentration camp, calling for Eliza Berlin to hurry.

And then take happiness where you can find it.

She ran.

She caught his hand.

And they boarded the train.

LESSON 73

Let yourself fall; I'll catch you
Lass dich fallen; ich fang dich auf

———

Elsa told the doctor that after the operation Herr K. gave her a necklace and a pearl ring, but she could see then—upon his face when he looked at her—a pained expression; was it guilt? No, she thought it was more accurately *distaste.* Elsa had lost her naïve charm.

Her affair with Herr K. ended badly.

She felt terrible pity for herself. And it was at this time that a friend—a married lady—began to offer consolation. And Elsa very soon was caught up and entangled in an odd and thrilling *amour.* Who was this lady? Elsa would not reveal her lover's name. The doctor was certain that the married lady in question was Magda Kaufmann. Hadn't Elsa long longed for her father's mistress? Hadn't Elsa often sighed over the sight of Magda's adorable white body? Elsa said that this mystery lady was devoted to her. They had a secret place where they stashed notes to each other; at first it was only a game. But the lady was possessive. The lady had such wants. Elsa, breathless, began to feel suffocated. There was too much hunger. Too much desire. It was maddening. Elsa could not move. And she did not know how to break free! Oh! It was true; Elsa was captivated. There was no world but theirs. And then things took a turn.

Things always take a turn.

Elsa met a young man. He was proper and polite; oh, how could he imagine the things she had done and felt and knew? He was innocent. And when she was with him; she too felt young and innocent. And Elsa—who had been taught at the forest's edge by Herr Kaufmann how not to say *no;* who had been etherized upon a doctor's table; and was taken up as pet by a beautiful married lady who devoured her—yes, yes—with kisses—admitted that it was nice to walk in the park with a boy and notice the birds or the snow and swap jokes and not worry too much about dreams and symbols and fears and what might happen if the worst came to it—which she was quick to qualify—*it would.* But one day the lady saw her with the young man. The lady too was walking in the park and spied her dear Elsa arm and arm with—

The lady grew angry and dark with tears and accused Elsa of—

Elsa could not find the word.

Infidelity? said the doctor.

No.

Deceit?

No.

Betrayal?

She shook head.

Of, she said. *being heartless.*

So, said the doctor, *it must have been soon after this that you lost sense of your arm?*

I suppose it was, she said.

And the young man? What became of him? asked the doctor.

She said, *He was not so innocent as I had thought.*

And what became of the lady? he asked.

She sends me letters. Not sends—no—she hides them yet in our secret place. I know where to look. I find them. I must—I have to burn them in the grate before mother gets hold of them, said Elsa.

So you look for these letters?

201

I do.
Why?
Because I know that they are there.
What does she want? asked the doctor.
Said the girl, *She wants—She wants. It is all that she knows, to want.*

LESSON 74

Get out of bed, it's already late!
Heraus aus dem Bett, es ist schon spät!

———

Elsa dreamed.

I am lost in the rooms of a palace. I find a dog. Poor thing! So skinny and ragged. The palace is desolate; the castle is in ruins. I run from room to room. There is a fire in the kitchen. The kitchen is on fire. Upon the table there is a spoon, a boot, and a noose. I take the rope and make a leash for the dog. I am looking for the stairs. Where are the stairs? We must get out of the palace before something terrible happens. A child appears and grabs onto both of my arms, tight, I can feel myself struggling to break free. I drop the rope. The dog runs. I see then that the roof is leaking. And that the bowls set out on the floor to catch the rainwater are overflowing. Even as the palace is flooding, the fire spreads. Where are the stairs? Where is the way out? The fire is continuing to spread.

And she confessed to the doctor, that it was here, just as she frantically searched for an exit, that she awoke—choking, coughing—to the distinct odor of burning.

LESSON 75

The pine tree had to be cut down
Die Kiefer musste gefällt werden

———

The doctor walked Elsa through her dreams symbol by symbol.

He began with the dream of the funeral.

He read from his tablet.

I am going to a funeral. I am wearing a white dress. And I don't want to go inside the chapel, because everyone is wearing black. And I have forgotten to wear black. The women are wearing beautiful black dresses and hats pinned with violets, but my white dress is shapeless, like a pilgrim's sack. And the man at the door tells me that I must go in; he says: This way! Hurry please! *But I don't want to go inside and instead I run.*

This represented her envy over her sisters' marriages. For she longed to marry Herr Kaufmann and to wear the bridal white. And yet the marriage she longed for had become a funeral. This was the funeral of the child.

Elsa asked, *What about the man? The man at the door telling me to hurry?*

Said the doctor, *He is the voice of reason telling you to look to the future; to give up your selfishness, your erratic and wild impulses. You must abandon your past in order to live a healthy life; this desire is at war—does battle with your fears of—your hunger for—being consumed—*

By whom?

By what, he corrected. *By desire itself.*

Asked Elsa, *May I tell you what I think the dream means?*

Elsa said, *It is a funeral; many people have died. Everyone is dead. Mother, Father, Martha, Theodor, Berit—everyone! But I am wearing white, because I have lived. It is an ugly uncomfortable dress, because I wish that I had died as well.*

Said the doctor, *Your interpretation of the dream is still part of the dream itself.*

It hasn't ended? she asked.

How could it? he said. *It doesn't end because you wake.*

She said, *The man is telling me to hurry, that I can still follow the others—*

Do you see, asked the doctor, *that you dream of death as a solution to your own problems? As a way to control your own little world?*

No, said the girl. *It isn't so. It isn't me. I don't believe you.*

The doctor did not advocate dreamers trying to understand their own dreams.

Let's move on, he said. *To the dream of the journey.*

He read.

We are traveling on a train at night in the dark. Not we, but I. I am in a dark compartment. The train stops. I get off at an unfamiliar station. It is snowing. I see Father and Theodor walking ahead along a road into a town. I call after them, but they do not hear me. I follow them, but I cannot seem to catch up. They are so far away. No matter how fast I follow, they do not get closer. I stumble over an open suitcase lying in the snow. It is full of gold coins. There are so many that I cannot count them. I can no longer see Father or Theodor; where have they gone? When I look down again, the suitcase is not full of coins but gold teeth. Where are Father and Theodor? I drag the suitcase; it is so heavy. I drag along the suitcase through the snow and keep walking even though it is dark and cold and I don't know where I am going.

The train was her erotic desire; the train took her to a dark and foreign place where she longed after her father and brother. When she

205

left the train, she found the open suitcase not full of coins but teeth—this was her guilt. She dragged the suitcase along with her because she was unwilling to relinquish her guilt; this: her valuable treasure she wanted, she hoarded—she kept even though it was too heavy—

The suitcase! she cried out.

The suitcase, she said, *I must keep it; I must carry it because it contains proof of—*

He said, *You refuse to understand the difference between right and wrong.*

Elsa said, *I will be separated from the people—and places—I know and once knew. I will be lost. I will lose even the things I hate.*

He wanted her to see how the symbols were beginning to fall into place; each image laying the path to decrypting the next dream.

She shook her head.

Doctor, she said. *The problem with these dreams is that they will come true.*

There is yet one more dream to consider, he said.

He gave her words back to her.

I am lost in the rooms of a palace. I find a dog. Poor thing! So skinny and ragged. The palace is desolate; the castle is in ruins. I run from room to room. There is a fire in the kitchen. The kitchen is on fire. Upon the table there is a spoon, a boot, and a noose. I take the rope and make a leash for the dog. I am looking for the stairs. Where are the stairs? We must get out of the palace before something terrible happens. A child appears and grabs onto both of my arms, tight, I can feel myself struggling to break free. I drop the rope. The dog runs. I see then that the roof is leaking. And that the bowls set out on the floor to catch the rainwater are overflowing. Even as the palace is flooding, the fire spreads. Where are the stairs? Where is the way out? The fire is continuing to spread.

She—her body—was the ruined palace. She had the choice of three objects: the boot, the noose, and the spoon. Why had she taken the noose? The boot was practicality; the spoon was compassion. Elsa wanted and feared the result of her affair with Herr K. She wanted the child, but feared it. The noose was not death, but pleasure; her pleasure in pain and despair. The dog was desire; she had tried to tame and rope it, but it would not be caught. When she dropped the rope, she saw the child who held onto her; she could not break free of the child. The flood of water was the birth. Her hunger could not be contained. The fire was an impossible urge. The fire was spreading.

These three dreams tell to me a story, he said.

The doctor lighted his pipe.

She said, *I see nightmares—fires, destruction—broken glass—your own house—*

Do you see, he said, *what adventurers we are, traveling into this strange place. Do you see that you are not alone? That we make our way together? I am here with you on this journey!*

She said, *I do not see. I cannot—*

He said, *In each dream you run, you are running—you are fighting to break free from the past and move on to the future.*

Elsa said, *I hate the future.*

He said, *Only because you wish to control it. Give up!*

He said, *Surrender!*

She turned from him.

She buried her face into the cushions of the sofa.

You, he said. *It is* you *who want disaster. You crave destruction. You wish and long for catastrophe!*

*The Germans—*she cried.

You! Not the Germans! he accused with pointed finger. *You!*

She was crying.

*But it is I who must tell you—*he went on—*I, who must make you see—you don't have that power; you cannot will a disaster into happening. No matter how frightening, remember; these are wishes; these are fears; wants; these are not visions, not signs and wonders. Your dreams are not real.*

She turned toward him; her pale face streaked with tears.

He said, *We cannot foretell events; the little world of your dreams is ordered by—symbols—subject to scrutiny, to interpretation—*

Oh no no, she cried. *The problem with my dreams is that—they will—in one way or another—come true!*

He demanded, *Why have you come to me? Is it to be healed? Do you trust me? Are you ready to move forward? This is the only way forward. This is the way to the future. You are locked in a ruined palace, and this is the only way out.*

She wept.

He waited.

She held a handkerchief to her eyes.

How dark outside the windows.

She could cry no more.

She was silent.

He smoked on in silence.

She was quiet.

It was time to go. How late it had gotten. It was late.

She was tired.

You should leave Berlin, she said.

He asked, *What have I to fear from your dreams?*

She did not answer.

Choose the future over the past, he said.

How else, he asked, *will we be able to travel this road together?*

He was not daunted. No, no, the doctor was pleased. For Elsa had finally showed progress. He knew that she would come to understand and to accept his interpretation of her dreams. The key fit the lock. It did. It would. It must.

One only fears the unknown; what one understands, after all, can no longer haunt or do harm.

LESSON 76

Do I ask too many questions?
Stelle ich zu viele Fragen?

⁓

Elsa Z. visited Dr. Apfel in his office for three months.

She confided. She told; she confessed strange and perverse longings. Desires, unspeakable. Acts, unmentionable.

What progress they were making.

Until one day her symptoms, she said, suddenly vanished.

She arrived in high spirits on the afternoon of what would be her
last visit. That morning she awoke to find full use of her hand.

The doctor was dubious.

The doctor did not believe—

It has happened like this, she told him. *Three days ago when I left
this house, I was met on the street by a friend—my secret beau—the one
of whom the married lady had been so jealous; remember?—and we
walked the zoological gardens. What strange birds there were in the winter sky! Have you seen the doves? They sit like spies in the plum trees. We
walked; he and I. As we made our way, we saw from the distance two
figures approaching; it was a girl and a young soldier. The soldier had
one hand in his pocket, and with the other he held the girl's gloved hand.
I thought: how very much in love they seem. Perhaps I was envious. And
then as the two drew still closer, I was certain that I saw—the twilight
was damp and hazy; the sky full of those dark-winged blackbirds—that
his hand was not in his pocket. I saw that the sleeve of his coat was*

pinned up. I was awfully sad. I felt awful for having been envious. He must have lost the limb on the battlefield. I could see in my mind's eye the makeshift hospital with its horrible knives and saws. I could smell the iodine and so much blood. I nearly swooned on the path. My beau took my arm to steady me. Here I thought: the girl with the soldier, what an angel she must be! Perhaps she had waited out the war for him, pining and worrying, and now—she was happy to have her sweetheart home—injured, but home. As the couple approached nearer still, my beau said: Look, it's Walter! I haven't seen him in ages. *And he raised a hand to wave in greeting. And the soldier, this Walter fellow, while still holding the girl's hand; he raised his other hand and called back:* Hello!

Elsa's eyes widened as she told her story.

He raised his arm!

The soldier's jacket had not been pinned up at the sleeve; he had only kept in military fashion, one arm behind his back as he walked. Elsa said that just then she was spent; exhausted, she could no longer bear the strange winter birds or her lover's company; she could not stop wondering about the girl, and if she had written letters to the soldier while he was away, or whether they had only just met. A light snow began to fall, and Elsa abruptly took leave of her own young man, went home; to her room—took to bed—without even taking tea. She spent two days with fever, but on the morning of the third day, she awoke to find her paralysis undone.

I am healed! she announced.

And she held out her hands to him.

LESSON 77

When I see the sea, I am happy
Wenn ich die See sehe, bin ich glücklich

———

—How cold it had been that winter—Anna recalled; Father and
Mother and Franz and Anna at home, sitting together—and for the
last time—in the parlor. Anna was restless and she went to the window—ducked between the closed curtains—to look out; but the
street was dark and empty. In the garden—a pall of snow—no more
apples or roses. Anna listened to Father. Father and Franz were talking—no, no, Father was—lecturing—while Franz, his head tilted
back against the sofa; he was trying to keep from dozing off—about
the boy's future. He was now twenty years old, and still nearly as
much of a child as Anna herself. What would he do? Had he plans?
Father worried. Didn't Franz see what was happening in the world?
Franz's mouth drooped slightly open as he began to drift into dream.
Mother sat beside her stepson. Anna hid behind the drawn curtains.
Father was growing cross. When Father was cross, he became sad
and solemn; it was his duty to teach his children. Their faults were
his faults. He must tell them, *us*, how to live, how to be and to do;
how to be just and fair and right. Poor Franz! He was falling asleep.
He tried to keep his eyes open and his ears interested, but how good
Dolfi's cake had been, and how nice and warm the room was! Father
taught; but Franz could not learn. Father was vexed. Madame
Madeline saw; she watched; her fingers occupied in needlework, she

turned in her seat and said to her husband, *Dearest, I heard the funniest little story the other day.*

The doctor paused in his lesson.

Franz woke.

Falki lifted his head from the floor.

Anna's little face poked out through the curtains.

Mother said, *Louis XV wanted to test the wit of one of his courtiers of whose talent he had been told. At the first chance he commanded the gentleman to tell a joke of which he, the king, should be the* sujet. *The courtier at once made the clever reply, "Le roi n'est pas sujet!"*

Madame, delighted, laughed.

Father set his spoon upon saucer.

Anna remembered the sound always and after.

It rang silvery.

And then fell dull.

Dr. Jozef Apfel set spoon upon his saucer.

Franz scuffled his boots on the floor.

Anna caught her fingers—knotting and unknotting—the curtains' roped velvet sash.

The room—hush, hush—went silent.

For Mother had told a joke.

And no husband was ever more certain of the symbolism of his wife's betrayal.

LESSON 78

A butterfly landed on his hand
Ein Schmetterling setzte sich auf seine Hand

———

What did Anna see?

When Elsa had her fit and fell from the piano bench, Madame Madeline screamed. And Franz came running. Anna stood watching from the doorway. The doctor was out. The doctor was—at that exact moment—delivering a lecture to his students on the topic of *How do we know what we know? An examination of Oedipus and the popular detective novel as related to the interrogative psychotherapeutic technique.* Madame screamed; Franz came running. Madeline fanned the girl's face. Tulla found smelling salts. Dolfi brought a cold compress. Franz lifted Elsa from the floor and placed her on the sofa. And Madame told Franz to take the girl home. Madame told Franz: *She is yours; take her away from my sight.*

And after that—

Anna did not see Elsa for some time. She knew that the lady in the little hat and the big gentleman who came to the door one day were Elsa's parents. When Elsa came to the house again, it was not to play piano with Maman. She came to be seen by Father.

What didn't Dr. Apfel know?

His son Franz had fallen in love with Elsa.

213

What did Dolfi not tell anyone but Tulla?

She didn't let on about Madame Madeline and Elsa embracing in the parlor.

What didn't Tulla tell anyone but Dolfi?

About Franz and Elsa kissing in the kitchen.

What did Madame Madeline know?

Elsa confessed to Madeline about Herr Kaufmann at the cottage by the woods where wildflowers grew; and how she had scratched and cried, to no avail; the first time. And then she gave in. *Poor sweet child!* consoled Madame Madeline.

What did the doctor call his son?

A daydreamer.

What did Tulla tell Dolfi?

How Madame Madeline and Elsa had a terrible row! Before Elsa fell into her fit—Madame had accused the girl—of infidelity. For Madame was jealous. Madeline said she had seen Elsa with—of all people! Franz! Elsa must tell her; Elsa must confess! Where did her true affections rest? Or was she even capable of such a thing as love? Tulla, scrubbing the hallway floors, heard. She heard Elsa imploring. Madame remained unmoved; Madeline would not believe her. Elsa pleaded at the piano bench. Madame would not relent. *You've broken my heart,* she said. Madame pushed Elsa away. And Elsa fell. She fell from the piano bench—and into a fit—a seizure—like one possessed! And Madame screamed for help. And Franz came running. *What have you done to her?* he said. But Madame said nothing. Elsa opened her eyes. And she cried out. She could not feel her arm. She could not move her hand. What happened? What has happened? Elsa is ill. Elsa fell; Elsa had fallen.

What did Anna hear Tulla tell to Dolfi?

How odd it was that Elsa should become Father's patient. For everyone in the house knew what Father did not.

What did Tulla and Dolfi know?

There were three entrances to the old house: there was the big front door, the kitchen steps, and around the winding back through the garden gate and around to the doctor's office. Franz in his coat awaited Elsa after she left the doctor; Franz standing in the snow, waiting by the gate.

What did Franz know?

Elsa saw in her dreams: boots, shoes, lamps, hair, eyeglasses, the bodies of birds, broken glass, coat hangers, pots and pans, suitcases, books, forks and knives and spoons, baby blankets, rope and noose, dolls, dogs, dishes, clocks, teeth, fire, and fishes.

What did Anna know?

It was Father, and only on paper, who called the girl Elsa. He gave each of his patients a new name. Oh, it was for privacy, for protection. He called her Elsa Z. But to Anna the girl did not seem like much of an Elsa. To Anna: Elsa was always Charlotte Blau.

What did the doctor do?

When Madame told her joke. Even Falki paused wide-eyed to lift his regal head from the floor. The key turned in the lock. And the door sprung open. What lay inside Elsa's locked room? Beyond—through the doorway—Dr. Apfel saw his own little world in ruins. For he knew that the joke that infected his wife had come to her by way of his patient. And he knew that the married lady with terrible wants was his own marble-white Madeline; and the young man not so innocent as Elsa had supposed was his own Franzchen.

What—who—in the doctor's house was as it—she—seemed? Only dear little Anna. He must protect his daughter. He knew what must be done. He must make a choice: his son or his wife. Whom would he forgive? Who would be granted forgiveness?

Whom did the doctor choose?

The doctor sent his son away. Jozef Apfel banished the children, Franz and Charlotte, from his house. No more did they linger in the garden. No more did Franz wait in his woolen coat. No more did Charlotte recline upon the doctor's sofa clasping her arm. And Madame suffered. For though she and her husband never spoke again of Elsa, Madeline wrote letter after letter on pale blue paper. Her letters went unanswered. She had no address to which to send them. She wrote letters to Franz. She wrote letters to Charlotte. She crammed notes into the far stone wall of the garden. Where Charlotte had collected secret sweets before her piano lessons. But Madame's notes now stayed stuck between stones. For no more did Charlotte gather love letters into her handbag and read them—quickly—feverishly—before burning them up in the grate. Madame Madeline sat lonely at her window and waited for her darling's return. The doctor sent the children to Paris. And in his wrath, his jealously, his punishment, in their exile, Jozef Apfel saved his son's life.

Charlotte, alas, poor Elsa; he knew and named her.

She had always been beyond his power to save.

LESSON 79

I am for peace and against war
Ich bin für den Frieden und gegen den Krieg

─────

Dr. Apfel sent Franz to Paris.

What happened to each and every Apfel by dear and year?

Each generation succeeded the previous.

Each child learned to live with what came before.

Some learned their lessons better than others.

Anna grew up in the Berlin house.

Her mother played sad songs; her father wrote important books.

Anna never again saw her brother or the girl called Elsa Z.

When Anna was twenty-two she went to England. She had lived for a while in London, and then—oh, she had lived in one place after the next. She had had so many mysterious adventures; why she had even married a man named Marx!

But then you don't want to hear about that; do you?

Not when there are dreams to be discussed.

One day when the past seemed very far away—Anna Marx went to Berlin. And she began to dream of demons and devils and things of such strange device.

These dreams reminded her of black plums falling—

And the banging of the wrought-iron gate—

Of Franz and Elsa in the garden.

It was as though Father himself wanted Anna to tell the story.

217

Franz traveled on to America.

He had three daughters.

Amalie Apfel cried on her wedding day.

She married Mitchell Leopold. She was an unhappy bride. She took solace in the fact that she was not so different from other unhappy brides.

Her story does not end here.

You can't imagine that it would end *here;* could you?

She fell in love with a primatologist who asked her to run away with him.

Of course; she didn't go with him.

Not when she had obligations, a son.

And then she had a daughter—

Amalie Leopold took her daughter Lemon to Hollywood.

And Lemon became a star.

A star! Well, such a thing is really only a symbol.

Lemon had the ability to be just where she should be.

Ben Leopold, the doctor, inherited history: he saw ghosts.

Hedy Apfel saw ghosts.

She couldn't escape them. No matter where she went—her ghosts followed. She heard them. Their fingers at the windowpanes.

Hedy took too many sleeping pills. She died. And everyone said that it was an accident. Although no one really believed that it was an accident.

No one disbelieved it, either.

Her husband was called Berlin.

Though there was nothing particularly German about him.

His name was a place.

To which he would never go.

Instead he had an antique shop.

In which all the clocks rang the wrong time.

Petra Apfel fell in love with Samuel Berlin.

She moved into his house. She took care of his child. And with hammer and nails: she hung the portrait of Dr. Jozef Apfel.

And Dr. Apfel watched over the family.

The family awaited his judgment.

The family is awaiting his judgment.

Amalie confessed her secrets to Petra.

And in the kitchen, Petra told Eliza stories.

And Eliza listened to Petra's stories.

The spoon turned round and round in the bowl.

Butter, eggs, flour: no story began or ended.

The oven timer ticked eternity.

Eliza grew and she learned.

But you don't really want to hear about what she learned; do you?

Not when there is chocolate cake to be eaten.

And ghost stories to be told.

Ben Leopold wanted to help his patients. He had explained his patients' ghost stories as symbolic manifestations of unconscious desires. His own ghosts were not so easily appeased.

His own ghosts traveled by train.

And braved such dark days between stations.

That it became difficult for Ben to understand what was real and what was not.

But then, you don't really want to hear about reality; do you?

Ben saw a girl in a brown dress drinking tea with his grandfather.

Lemon longed for the perfect story.

Eliza fell for fanatics.

Dr. Apfel tried for five years to write *The Case of Elsa Z.*

He began it; and tore the pages up. He crossed out words. He interpreted her dreams; his own dreams; his interpretation of his interpretation. He asked questions that he dared not answer. And when he received word in August 1925, on that sunny day; when

Anna tossed the ball to Tulla. When Madeline sat beneath her sunshade. When the black plums ripened and fell from the boughs and rolled across the lawn to be captured by Dolfi and collected in her basket. When they were—the Apfels at home—as happy as Germans. When the doctor sitting in his office among his statuettes of terra-cotta gods and marble goddesses; at his desk looking out his window; opened a letter from his son; and read about the death of Franz's beautiful young wife.

Charlotte Blau died in Paris.

It was influenza.

That August day the doctor wrote—as he remembered it—Elsa's case.

He did not complete his analysis.

The king is never a subject.

Madame Madeline accepted her punishment.

LESSON 80

The ice will no longer bear any weight
Das Eis wird nicht mehr tragen

―――――

Do you recall maps and apricots? A butter more buttery? A Berlin more bellicose? A less dogmatic God? A girl like Eliza? A boy like Hart? Do you remember? Dreams and their relation to the unconscious? Hart heard boots marching in time on every street corner. The ineffable blondes; the pie-faced children; the good neighbors: the foreign, the familiar. Hart and Eliza: they had learned history from the movies.

Whom could such a history help?

They traveled by train on a day in November to Sachsenhausen, to see the camp.

To Oranienburg: just north of Berlin.

They almost missed the train.

Hart wanted to go, but Eliza did not.

She could not take on this kind of reality face- and fist-first.

She was not brave or fantastic.

The day was cold.

The train arrived at the station.

They had still a long way to walk.

The rain turned to snow.

It began to snow.

They had had a late start of things—the train ride, the long walk; they would only just make it to Sachsenhausen before the gate was locked and closed for the day. Hart looked at his watch. *Run*, he said. They ran.

Have you ever seen the falling snow in Germany?

There is nothing more beautiful.

Hart was running.

He could not catch his breath.

He passed through the gate.

He hurried—he knew where he wanted to go—he needed to find the place that had been called Station Z.; he wanted to get there; to what now remained of it: the foundation.

The extermination chamber had long since been torn down.

The foundation remained.

He ran. She followed.

And then he stopped.

He was deep.

He was grave.

Hart fell to the ground.

Eliza fell to his side; she called out.

She cried: *Help!*

She cried: *Send for an ambulance!*

But there were no other visitors at the concentration camp at the closing hour on that day in November. A man from the museum came out and rushed back inside and made a phone call.

By the time the ambulance arrived, it was too late.

And so Hart died.

Not with a bang but a missed beat.

His heart—a name; a punch line—it had never been right.

He survived the miracle of his own birth for only so long.

His heart stopped.

The snow fell from that German sky of blue down upon the concentration camp.

Hart called out to God.

He was in a hurry to get in one last question.

The ambulance arrived.

In the hospital everyone was helpful—the doctors, the nurses; wanted to help the Jewish boy named Hart whose crazy heart had stopped—Where?—

Get him home. Find his home. Send the body home; bury him.

His death was a spectacle.

It was an impossibility.

It was an implausibility.

It was an improbability.

Send him home.

His body was a reminder.

Do you remember? It is too much to remember.

LESSON 81

We walked through a big park, a dark forest, and high grass

Wir sind durch einen grossen Park, einen dunklen Wald, und hohes Gras gegangen

———

Eliza had an abortion.

LESSON 82

Don't get so annoyed! Try to see the humorous side of it!
Sei nicht so wütend! Nimm die Sache lieber mit Humor!

———

Because Eliza had so far been unlucky, this did not mean that at any moment her luck might not change. There had even been a brief era, a tiny epoch, as small as a cemetery or as large as a thumbtack, when she was run off her feet by fortune. When it came to her—the thought— that she had never inhabited a world that did not contain Hart Luther.

This only made it that much worse when she had to go on in a world without him.

What would have happened if they had never gone to Berlin?

Would things have been different?

Eliza wrote romance novels.

She called herself Justine St. Ives.

Because terrorism is love.

And love is structured like a language.

German is not a romance language, but one can still speak of oceans and opium fields; the slave trade; drought, famine and flood; Donald Duck and Dracula; of libraries and dictionaries and rolled dice; and describe as well, in very accurate terms, the smoke of oil and ash and flesh and fat and candle. Maybe tomorrow a bomb would explode. Or a bird would fly from a branch. Maybe a mystery will be revealed; a heart broken; a code cracked. And a flag unfurled. Maybe Eliza would stay in Germany; and she would learn the language.

LESSON 83

His watch has stopped
Seine Uhr ist stehengeblieben

———

How romantic was Justine St. Ives?

Oil lamp, candelabra, or candle? What lighted the room in which Lizette waltzed with the dashing dauphin? Did they ride home from the ball in a phaeton sleigh? Was Genevieve virtuous or a vixen? Whom did Bethany betray? Caroline in her corset and crinolines awaited Pierre on the veranda at the old plantation. The morning was sweet with wild rose and magnolia blossoms. Dressed in Wimbledon white, Julia offered herself with abandon upon the velveteen divan in the library to Wilder; oh Wilder! Who did what to whom down in the wine cellar while upstairs a dull dinner party dragged on? Who burgled Bonnie up against the wall in the bank vault? In the cloister who confessed to Sister Katherine? Who made hay with Helmut at dawn in the dewy fields? How many breasts unbodiced? How many rounded thighs exposed a shy garter? How many buckskin britches unbelted in the barn? How many *heaves* and *sobs* and *sighs* and *whispers* and *hushes* and *hopes?* How many *trysts, tumults,* and *tumbles?* What of *assignations* and *imbroglios?* So much fog, mist, and moonlight. How many dreamy Desdemonas were wooed with a sword? How many cities sacked for the favor of a fickle Helen? How many gods begot new gods with the ravishing of a ready Gretchen? How many fevered testimonies heard in the back

226

row of the revivalist's tent? How many cops clutched nightsticks in hot pursuit of a jewel thief? How many kisses stolen behind the potted palm in the hotel lobby? How many tear-stained cheeks aglow as the airplane taxied the runway? How many young brides clasped their dying husbands in their arms? How many feels copped in the kitchen while the rack of lamb roasted? How many *swollen mouths* and *stunned silences* and *retreating footsteps?* How much breathless anticipation? How many Sirens serenaded sailors as ships sank at sea? How many trains *zug, zug, zug* chugged along as snow fell on a landscape rapidly diminishing into darkness?

LESSON 84

Each box contains five bars of soap
Jede Schachtel enthält fünf Stück Seife

What did Anna remember?

It was hard to imagine a world without Mother, her black hair pinned up, her back to you at the piano, her fingers playing on the keys. It was hard to imagine a world without Father, who taught his children the difference between right and wrong. It was hard to imagine a world without Tulla, who scorched the tablecloth when she did the ironing. It was hard to imagine a world without Father's patients: the gentlemen with walking sticks and the ladies in fur-collared coats who carried cinnamon candies in their handbags. It was hard to know a world without Dolfi. It was hard to understand a world without Aron, from the butcher's, who sang as he tossed bones to dogs in the snow. It was hard to know a world without Franz, who kissed Charlotte in the kitchen. There were two cats. And a dog named Falki. Father said: *This is no world for dreamers.* And Mother closed her eyes and moved her fingers up and down the ivory and black keys.

And then after a while, it was hard to imagine a world that once held Father and Mother.

It was hard to imagine that a girl like Tulla had ever existed.

Was there ever a brother like Franz, who daydreamed? Or Dolfi, who loved the cinema? Or Charlotte, who had a heart-shaped face?

It was hard to imagine a world.

Year by year other faces replaced those that had disappeared.

Until it was hard to remember Mother's face, only her black hair pinned up.

And one day the cats crept out of the broken window.

What happened to the dogs in the snow?

It became hard to imagine even the piano.

The snow: this was real; wasn't it?

And what about the piano?

LESSON 85

There is a large garden behind the house
Hinter dem Haus ist ein grosser Garten

———

Lemon, never plagued by poor sleep, unhappy memories, or bad dreams, awoke in the night. It took her a moment to recall: *I am in a hotel room. I am in a hotel in Berlin. I have woken in the night.* She fumbled for the lamp on the table. She found a pen—and on the hotel stationery—she began to write.

LESSON 86

We only want what's best for you
Wir wollen nur das Beste für euch

⸺

The time passed so quickly!

Has it been only a week?

And yet everything seems different.

How you have changed and grown—

Have you enjoyed Berlin?

Did you get a chance to visit Cologne, Munich, Dresden, Frankfurt, Nuremberg, Leipzig, or the Bavarian Alps?

What of Heidelberg, Bayreuth, and Stuttgart?

Or Bonn and Düsseldorf?

You learned new words; and tasted, touched, heard, smelled, and saw so very much!

Days when the sun broke through the clouds.

Dogs that barked in German!

Marble monuments to great men.

Cathedrals built long ago by hand, stone upon stone.

Their bare-breasted gargoyles grinning.

Beautiful women in black leather.

Exquisite automobiles.

People hurrying to and fro.

Poets and professors riding bicycles!

Pink-haired girls, pierced punks, skinheads, tattooed teenagers.

Fathers, mothers, children.

Happy lives; the marriage of art and science and technology!

Fables and forests.

One Germany! United under the flag, the eagle, and God.

Skyscrapers built of steel, glass, and metal; lovingly, maddeningly, exactly with exactitude constructed girder upon girder, up high and ever upward.

Crumbling concrete, sand, silt, stone, and dust.

Milk and cream and cheese and eggs and butter and almonds.

You said: *danke*. You smiled: *bitte*. In your *Kaffee* you took a spoonful or two of *Zucker*.

You asked questions. Whether they were answered or not, you asked.

And if you did not see and do absolutely all that you had hoped—?

You are sated.

So much cake!

So many sights.

Here Faust flew!

And the great black cape of Mephistopheles shrouded the sky!

You saw. Don't you now see?

All things are possible.

LESSON 87

I like people with fair hair
Mir gefallen Leute mit blonden Haaren

———

What is the problem with Germans?

Once upon a time in Berlin there lived a girl called Charlotte Blau. She was young and beautiful. One day she abandoned her home for Paris. She loved and was loved. And her life ended in disaster. This is not the whole of her story. She had dreams and visions. She said: *Something terrible is going to happen.* No one believed her. Her father did not believe her. Her mother did not believe her. Her sisters and brother did not believe her. You would have to be crazy to believe her. Are you crazy? Why should anyone listen to her ravings? She had a history of histrionics. Her father and mother brought her on a day in autumn too warm for the season to the office of the esteemed Dr. Apfel. To him jokes were no laughing matter. He took her case; he renamed Charlotte in his notes for the purpose of privacy: Elsa Z. She led him through a maze of symptoms and discontents. She could not move her arm. She coughed and complained. Her father had a mistress. Her mother was obsessive; her mother could not rid herself—through cleaning, scrubbing, and praying—of the past. Elsa had an affair with a married man. The affair began not too happily. The doctor told Elsa that she was bound to feel two ways about the rape and romance. The doctor said that the girl felt desire and guilt. Elsa got into trouble. Her father's mistress helped her to get an abortion. Elsa said that she did not regret her operation because she had seen terrors beyond imagination in her dreams. The doctor said that nothing is beyond imagination. The doctor said that there is no *no* in the unconscious mind. Only *yes* and *yes* and *yes*. And he unwound the skein and found his way through her dreams symbol by symbol. And so her case sprung open easily as a picklock. But wait! Before Dr. Apfel could complete his work, the girl claimed to be healed. And she held her hands out to him. See? He saw. Elsa never again came to the doctor. The doctor realized that his palace was in ruins; the fire was continuing to spread. His wife and son shared a secret. They loved Elsa. It was hard not to love Elsa. Madame Madeline pined; Franz did not protest when his father banished him. And Franz and Charlotte-called-Elsa married in Paris; they had a wedding portrait shot. Anna found this picture when she was fifteen and searching through her father's office; she found it in the file along with the unfinished inconclusive *Case of Elsa Z.* Anna learned that day the worst lesson: her father did not know everything. His definitions were not definitive. Franz and Charlotte faced the camera. How many brides were quite so beautiful as was she? Or young husbands as devoted? And in how many likewise time-frayed photographs does a girl on her wedding day sit, gloved hands bouquet clasping—forever future facing—while a groom stands behind her? They spent nearly four years in Paris. Charlotte dreamed nightly; each dream worse than the next. She grew weak. When she took ill with influenza she fell into ravings. *The Germans*—Germany was far away, but Charlotte cried out. Franz could not leave Charlotte by herself. Once he left her sick bed for only a moment and when he returned, Charlotte in her nightdress was trying to throw herself from the window. Franz found a girl who could speak German to sit with her. The girl was named Margot. Charlotte's fever worsened; Charlotte died. From then on Margot took care of Franz. Because she was young. And because he had lost his mind. And because she knew that love is obligation. Margot had listened to Charlotte, to her predictions. Charlotte had made Margot promise to take Franz away. And after Charlotte died, Franz and Margot took a ship—sailed—to America. And Margot promised more: she would never speak of what she had learned from Charlotte Blau. Margot kept the past a secret. Because after all, it was impossible to make real the destruction of a world: to recall each thief and lunatic. Each dream and each dreamer. And those too whose lives had been extraordinarily ordinary. Not to mention *Objekts:* each fallen plum and piano and postcard. So on to America went Franz and Margot. Where no one gave a thought to the past. Where the future was *the thing*. And Franz worked in a bakery; for he had learned from Dolfi in his father's house the mysteries of sugar and salt. He became expert at wedding cakes. And it was thought— rumored—that his cakes brought good luck to young couples starting out together in life. He constructed lovingly, maddeningly, rose-bedecked cakes layer upon layer, up high and ever upward; and there at the top of each buttercream monument stood two perfect marzipan ghosts: a tiny bouquet-bearing bride and her almond-sweet dream-dazed groom. Arm in arm: together. Margot married Franz, and they had three daughters called Amalie, Hedy, and Petra. None of whom ever knew that their father had been married first to a girl named Charlotte Blau, who had been called Elsa Z.

What is more romantic than genocide?

Anna finished her story.

LESSON 88

All dreams don't come true
Alle Träume erfüllen sich nicht

───────

Anna had finished telling her story.

The trees were bare. The day was diminishing.

Lemon and Eliza sat with their great-aunt.

"We were not so different from other families," said Anna.

They had not been, had they?

They were not, were they?

So different?

Three teacups emptied.

The last of the sugar spooned.

It was time to go.

Eliza waited for the last lesson.

Lemon longed for a dramatic conclusion.

"Tell me one thing," said Lemon. "The riddle—"

"The riddle?" asked Anna.

Lemon said, "What is greater than the universe? What is it that the dead eat, but if the living do, they will die?"

"Oh," said Anna. "Don't you know?"

Eliza did not know.

Lemon didn't know.

"Nothing," said Anna.

It was evening. It was snowing.

And it was going to snow.

When Lemon and Eliza walked outside they found that the world had turned hard and cold and ice-bright.

LESSON 89

The astronauts' mission is to discover how large the ozone hole in
the atmosphere is
*Die Astronauten sollen auf ihrer Mission untersuchen, wie gross das
Ozonloch in der Atmosphäre ist*

———

Snow fell and was falling that evening upon the darkened windows
of the old Apfel house.

Lemon and Eliza knew the way. The path lay before them; they
walked the path. Lemon unlatched—opened—the garden gate.
Snow fell upon the stones and covered white the flowerbeds. Winter
birds sat in the limbs of the cedar trees.

This house was all that was left in Berlin to see.

Lemon stared up at the great ruined palace.

Eliza went to the wall at the garden's edge.

She pressed her hands, cold and bare, against the stones.

Days of rain had left the garden—alive, awake, awaiting—
strange. Roses clung to the branch; grapevines tangled damp, brown,
root-rotting. By morning—gone—frozen; the garden would be
blanketed in snow.

Lemon stared at the house.

She heard a piano playing. Not a lamp was lit. And not a light
shined out.

Eliza went to her knees before the stone wall.

Lemon closed her eyes.

She heard music—voices—

She felt such shadows in the cold—

There were shapes and whisperings and shadows.

She nearly fell; she almost swooned.

She wanted—she wanted—to escape—

For she knew—of a sudden—that they were not alone in the winter garden.

They were surrounded; so many eyes fell upon them, from every window they looked out, gazed, watched, waited: Tulla and Dolfi; the doctor in his study; his wife in her punishment pining in the parlor; Franz and Elsa peered out caught in mid-caress from the kitchen.

Lemon called to Eliza—

Let's go. Let's go.

It was time to go.

Lemon in her scarf and woolen coat and leather gloves went to Eliza.

Eliza knelt in the snow.

Eliza kneeling at the wall; she turned her face up to look at Lemon.

Eliza held her cold wet raw hands curled into fists out to Lemon.

It was snowing. The snow fell and fell. And the wind blew the branches of the trees, which scratched fingers against the house: *Let me in, let me in!* Eliza opened her fists to reveal ragged scraps of folded paper, the ink long since faded, run away; her hands open; she opened her hands and the paper was lifted up—captured, caught—on the cold unforgiving wind the bits of blue paper blew from Eliza's opened palms to scatter across the garden and up up up flew flying their way skyward. Eliza opened her fists and her palms were empty.

LESSON 90

There are circus posters everywhere
Überall hängen Zirkusplakate

———

Justine St. Ives and Plum Peabody walked the Unter den Linden in the falling snow.

Justine was sad.

"Poor dear you," said Plum. "You wanted a happy ending."

"No, no," said Justine.

"Don't cry," Plum commanded.

"Tell me," said Plum. "What did you want?"

"I wanted——" said Justine.

"You wanted answers? You wanted punishment for the guilty?"

Said Justine, "I wanted——"

"You hoped——" said Plum.

Justine said, "I did. I did. I had hope. I hoped——"

"That it might have been different?" asked Plum.

Said Justine, "Isn't there still a chance——?"

Asked Plum, "How much cake does a girl need?"

And they walked.

Plum asked Justine, "Have you heard this one? Two psychiatrists are drinking in a bar. One says to the other, 'What was your most difficult case?'

"The other replies, 'I had a patient who lived in a fantasy world. He believed that an uncle in South America was going to die and leave him a fortune. All day long my patient waited for a letter to arrive telling of his great inheritance. He never went out. He never did anything. He sat and stared at his mailbox and waited and waited for this imaginary letter from his imaginary uncle. I worked with this man for eight years.'

"'What happened?' asks the first doctor.

"'As I say, it was an eight-year struggle, but I finally cured him, and—'

"'And?' asks the first doctor.

"'And,' says the second doctor, 'Then that stupid letter arrived!'"

Plum laughed.

Justine pondered.

Snow fell.

A dog barked.

The ice shined like broken glass.

The lights of the city shimmered.

Plum grabbed Justine's hand and off they ran running.

They slipped. They slid. But they did not fall.

They ran.

LESSON 91

The German flag is black, red, and gold
Die deutsche Fahne ist schwarz, rot, gold

———

What happened to Hedy?

Hedy Apfel fell in love with Samuel Berlin when he introduced himself at her sister's wedding reception by saying: *My name is Berlin, and there is nothing particularly German about me.* It was late in the evening, and the remains of the cake were being parceled out and packed up for the girls and spinsters and maiden aunts to take home and place under their pillows to dream happily of men they would never marry. The bandleader settled up the bill with Jack Leopold. And Sam Berlin, standing behind Hedy, took hold of her elbow and whispered in her ear. And Hedy whispered back, without turning, with the slightest tilt of her head in the direction of her bare shoulder: *What's your name?*

What happened to Petra?

Petra Apfel fell in love with Samuel Berlin when she saw him before the wedding ceremony began; he sat smoking a cigarette in the garden behind the temple. Petra had escaped the dressing room—crowded with perfumed bridesmaids in various states of undress—to wander outside. And there he was, dark in his dark wool suit, sitting on a stone bench while all around, the roses began at once to bloom and the lilacs wither in the afternoon sun.

How did Hedy and Petra get home?

Now that you mention it, they walked. Hedy, barefoot, held her shoes by the heels in one hand and Petra's hand in the other. And it was a nice night, thick, hot, and starry. Petra held her flower girl's basket empty of flowers. And it wasn't a long walk. Hedy hobbled and Petra hopped in the darkness.

And after?

The band went home. The catering ladies went home; they took off their black dresses with white collars. They ate dinner with their husbands and children. They watched television. They listened to the radio. Some sat on stoops and porches, hoping for a breeze. Petra and Hedy walked home. They took off their tomato-red dresses in favor of thin summer nightgowns. They crawled into their twin beds in the room they shared. Hedy in the lamplight read aloud a story from a magazine. Petra heard most of it, but fell asleep before the end. The rabbi went home. The cantor went home. Hillel Brightman and Joan Schecter parked on a side street and in the backseat did everything *but*. Samuel Berlin and Fran Schecter, unfortunately, were sitting in the front seat at the time, trying to ignore the goings-on behind them. Fran talked about the intelligence of poodles. Sam stared out the window. He saw them—can you believe it? He saw Hedy and Petra walking on their bare hot feet in the moonlight. Dot and Jack Leopold went home. Everybody, everyone, everybody went home. They straggled. They meandered. They gave good-night kisses and were kissed in kind. They walked, drove, were dropped, were driven. They took buses and taxicabs. They took off fancy dresses and untied ties. They ate wedding cake with melting frosting rosettes. They bathed and brushed teeth. They talked about what would happen tomorrow and tomorrow and the next day. They dressed in pajamas and nightgowns. Some wore nothing at all. Some slept; others did not. Because it was hot. How hot was it? And it's hard to sleep, you have to admit, let alone dream, on hot summer nights. After Petra fell asleep, Hedy put down the magazine and opened her library-borrowed copy of *Wuthering Heights* and read until dawn.

LESSON 92

The gate is locked
Das Tor ist abgeschlossen

On a cold and sunny afternoon in November 1938, a brick crashed through the leaded glass pane of a window in Dr. Apfel's office. The brick tore the tapestry curtain down from the brass rod and landed on and smashed a rosewood table before falling dull upon the Persian rug. A sheath of unbound papers fluttered, flew, and fell to the floor. No one came in to clean up the mess.

LESSON 93

That tree has very deep roots
Der Baum hat sehr tiefe Wurzeln

———

A king during wartime visited a hospital and came upon a doctor carrying out the amputation of a soldier's leg. The king praised the doctor's skill with loud exclamations of royal satisfaction. *Bravo! Bravo! Dear Doctor!* When the operation was finished, the doctor approached the king and asked with a deep bow: *Is it your majesty's command that I should remove the other leg too?*

Eliza walked Berlin: past children running, girls queuing for buses. Past monuments of marble and stone and steel. Past skyscrapers and ruined palaces. She walked along orderly esplanades. It was winter. All the history in the world had already happened. Amid purposeful passersby going to work, riding bicycles in the snow, to the shops or the cinema. She lingered in Berlin; she saw trains arrive and depart. She saw doves in the bare branches of plum trees. She called the city her own. And nothing was beyond her imagination.

Ben Leopold sat by the pool in the darkness. He rose from his chair. He picked up the bottle. He picked up his glass. As he walked around the pool, he stumbled—just then over a stack of scripts. He fell over *Faust.* His glass had shattered; the bottle smashed. He got up. His hand was bleeding. In the house, in the kitchen, he washed his hands with soap and hot water. He bandaged his hand. He found himself in the kitchen. It was without thinking that he began. That he found a bowl. He found eggs and butter. He creamed the butter and sugar. He cracked the eggs. He added vanilla. He turned on the oven. He turned the spoon round and round in the bowl. He had only to want, and an ingredient appeared before him. He found flour and salt. He found all that he needed. Without knowing the nature of his need: chocolate and cherries; cocoa and kirsch. He measured. He mixed. He turned on the radio. It was a call-in show. A doctor was analyzing dreams. Ben had his cake in the oven. He knew what to do. How did he know what to do? How did he *know?* Ben sat at the table and listened to the dream doctor. He took the cake from the oven. It was beautiful. He had never seen anything more beautiful. Was there ever anything more beautiful than a Black Forest cake left to cool on a table? He fell asleep. He slept. He dreamed that there was no cake. There was no Black Forest. When he woke—in sunlight—the cake was on the table. The cake, if possible, had become more perfect. He mixed whipping cream, confectioner's sugar, chocolate, and coffee. He frosted the cake. He did not pick up the knife. He did not cut into the cake. It was perfect. He knew that it was perfect. He admired the cake for a moment. The sweet, the salt, the bitter. It was real. It was enough to know that it existed; that it continued to exist. And when it was gone, and there was no more of it; wouldn't it be enough to know that it had once existed? He left the cake for his sister. So that she would get the joke. No; he didn't take the cake. And then he left Lemon's house. Dr. Leopold's patients had dreams and nightmares. And Dr. Leopold had patients awaiting him.

Julia did not tell Wilder that she was going to have his child. When he left for his important work in the jungle, he asked her to come with him. He said that they could run away together. He told her to leave the past behind. And she in tears gave him her answer: *No!* Wilder left her. It was just then that Fielding suddenly dropped dead during a polo match; Julia, the young widow, looked exquisite in her black satin and mourning veil. Now she and Wilder could be together; but wait! It was too late! He had disappeared. Into the jungle. The worst was feared. Julia went in search of Wilder. She trekked through the thick of it to find him. She suffered heat and rain and dark nights with their child in a rucksack on her back. And just when hope was lost, she saw him! She found him. Do you see? His leg broken; she ran to him. They kissed under the canopy of branches and leaves, as the sun broke through the shimmering green, to the cheers *hooray hooray* of an audience of clamoring chimps.

Faustus—Dr. Faust—claimed to perform the miracles of Christ. Self-appointed and ale-anointed sixteenth-century demigod of inn, roadhouse, and tavern; swigger, swaggerer, astrologer, alchemist, fancier of necromancy, sodomite, soothsayer, seducer, and the seduced: he cast horoscopes and conjured the dead to rise. He sold himself to the devil for secret knowledge. He bragged of his magics to monks and wide-eyed willing barmaids: *I have gone further than you think and haved pledged myself to the devil with my own blood, to be his in eternity, body and soul.* Mephistopheles followed Faust down a dark alley. The devil disguised himself as a black poodle. Mephisto and Faustus flew hand in hand across the sky. The doctor did as he desired, dreamed, and more. He found finally the final solution to his earthly problems. And what of that moment at the end? Who claimed; who lay claim to Faust's soul? At the last moment the magus of Heidelberg repented. And he cried out: *I'll burn my books!*

Martin Luther was born on November 10, 1483. The story started, if you can believe it, in Germany: as a young man he was caught in a violent thunderstorm. He was nearly struck by lightning and thrown to the ground. He vowed to become a monk if he could escape the storm. In 1517, Martin Luther took up a hammer and posted his 95 Theses to protest the sale of indulgences. In 1525, he wrote *Against the Murderous and Thieving Hordes of Peasants*. He married a former nun, Katharina von Bora. She gave birth to six children. In 1543, he wrote *On the Jews and Their Lies*. In 1546, Martin Luther died. His death was attributed to heart failure.

Charlotte Blau in her brown dress walks upon the shore; Klara Apfel's black hair ribbons tangle in the wind, the hem of her white dress drags in the water; Madame Madeline carries a parasol. And little Anna is here too. Frau Frederika in an elegant hat and gloves shoos away pigeons, *filthy beasts!* Theodor carries a book and he reads as he walks; Herr Kaufmann studies his pocket watch, but what can time matter to him? He has no more trains to catch. He has no more appointments or dates to keep. Magda Kaufmann coos to Herr Karl Blau; Martha, Berit, Käthe, Greta, Fredi, and spoiled Stefan sift the sand for snails. Waves crash and tumble. What a perfect holiday, not a drop of rain in sight. If Hedy Berlin isn't careful, she will certainly get a sunburn! And who is that tall fellow who walks beside her? Look! There is Udo, the funny soldier, running right into the water; he is swimming in his uniform! Tulla and Aron bring the picnic baskets and blankets; Dolfi holds Anna by the hand; and there is the old doctor, in a banded straw hat and linen suit, feeding the birds, scattering breadcrumbs as he goes. This is a world reserved for dreamers. They trample on in the sand, laughing and arguing and fighting and scolding and telling stories. And last—lagging behind—oh, here comes Franz and his dog Hitler chasing after butterflies.

Cartaphilus, the storied Wandering Jew, appeared in Hamburg in 1542; Gibraltar in 1575; the Netherlands in the same year; Vienna in 1599; Lübeck in 1601; Prague in 1602; Rome in 1603; Bavaria in 1604;

seen sailing from Constantinople upon a ship with dark sails in 1610; seen in Ypres in 1623; Brussels in 1640; Leipzig, 1642; Paris in 1644; Stamford in 1658; Astrakhan in 1672; Frankenstein in 1676; Munich in 1721; appeared in Altbach in 1766; the Carpathian mountains in 1770; rumored found in St. Petersburg in 1774—when a thief sentenced to the gallows escaped before his hanging; and he then told all who would listen that it was the eternal Jew himself who had by night unlocked his cell with a key made of stone. The wanderer was spotted again in Newcastle, England, in 1790; at a train station. And then not seen again until in America in 1868. And here ended his trail. He was last sighted crossing the Great Plains in a wagon drawn by two pale horses. He was heading westward.

Lemon's next film, *Alphabet,* was box office boffo; which is to say: it was a hit. Audiences were stunned in the end when the final plot twist revealed that she was the serial killer. And just when the public craved—desired—needed—wanted her most, she became *private.* She refused interviews. She did not go to parties or premieres. Or wear the exquisite dresses offered to her by designers. What did she do? She sat by the side of her swimming pool, dangling her bare legs into the very blue water and there in longhand on unlined paper under the bright hazy California sun, she wrote a screenplay that she called: *The Avenue of Limes.* For she realized, yes, yes, she had grown up in Hollywood where all things are possible, and she had gone to Berlin; she went to Germany; she had eaten cake and said *please* and *thank you:* she was—she knew now, she had learned—the best person to tell the story of Dr. Apfel and Elsa Z.

LESSON 94

The bottle is empty; his glass is still full
Die Flasche ist leer; sein Glas ist noch voll

━━━━━

What is the problem with Jews?

Under that German sky of blue Hart fell to the ground, and he called out to God, the joiner of joints; diviner of dreams; the cleaver, the carper, the cardsharp who doubledealt diamonds and palmed hearts; God of dirt and ditch; stamen and pistil; surfeit, overplus, and aftermath; God the lamb, the ram, the hart, the liar, the loser, the loner, the lunatic, the heaper of wheat; the hoarder; the goat, the gobbler; the joker, the juggernaut; God the fanatic, the fascist, the carver of tablets and layer of laws; the mountebank and martyr; God the greenhorn, the grifter, the goofball; the boot, the noose, the spoon; the star; the sap; the ape; the pen; the plum; the plume; the past; the dupe; the kook, the creep; the collector and keeper; ash and candle; God climbing the ladder, wrestling, weeping, watching, waiting; that white-bearded old man with horns and hooves; God the jackass, the genius, the genesis; Hart asked him: *What happens next?*

LESSON 95

Time's up!
Die Zeit ist um!

───❦───

Leave Berlin; you really must.

Pack your bag; purchase your ticket.

Go home. Your plants want watering; the mail is piling up in the box.

Leave Berlin. The mattress is lumpy. Your feet hurt. You've gained eight pounds. How much cake does a girl need? You are tired of maps, marzipan, and museums. You are fed up with *Strudel* and *Schweinefleisch*. History has got you down. It is time to go home.

Go home; unpack your bag; turn the page of your calendar.

Look to the future! Go home for the baseball, hot dogs, and Coca-Cola. For the Hershey's bars. For Hollywood! For the new movies coming out and the ones that you missed while you were away. Sleep in your own bed; speak your own language.

Go about your life. Move faster. Move forward. Be brave and fantastic. Eat a peach; smell the flowers; climb every mountain; hug your kid; commit random acts of kindness; recycle, reuse, renew. Don't be a perpetrator; try not to be a victim; avoid being a bystander.

Imagine that there was never a place called Germany.

And that the symbols in your dreams mean only what you want.

Imagine that every place is called: Germany.

COLOPHON

German for Travelers was designed at Coffee House Press,
in the historic Grain Belt Brewery's Bottling House near downtown Minneapolis.
The text is set in Garamond.

FUNDER ACKNOWLEDGMENTS

Coffee House Press is an independent nonprofit literary publisher. Our books are made possible through the generous support of grants and gifts from many foundations, corporate giving programs, state and federal support, and through donations from individuals who believe in the transformational power of literature. This book was made possible, in part, through a special project grant from the National Endowment for the Arts, a federal agency. Coffee House receives major general operating support from the McKnight Foundation, the Bush Foundation, from Target, and from the Minnesota State Arts Board, through an appropriation by the Minnesota State Legislature and from the National Endowment for the Arts. Coffee House also receives support from: an anonymous donor; the Elmer L. and Eleanor J. Andersen Foundation; Bill Berkson; the James L. and Nancy J. Bildner Foundation; the Patrick and Aimee Butler Family Foundation; the Buuck Family Foundation; the law firm of Fredrikson & Byron, PA.; Jennifer Haugh; Anselm Hollo and Jane Dalrymple-Hollo; Jeffrey Hom; Stephen and Isabel Keating; the Kenneth Koch Literary Estate; Seymour Kornblum and Gerry Lauter; the Lenfestey Family Foundation; Ethan J. Litman; Mary McDermid; Rebecca Rand; the law firm of Schwegman, Lundberg, Woessner, PA.; Charles Steffey and Suzannah Martin; Jeffrey Sugerman; Stu Wilson and Mel Barker; the Archie D. & Bertha H. Walker Foundation; the Woessner Freeman Family Foundation; the Wood-Rill Foundation; and many other generous individual donors.

NATIONAL
ENDOWMENT
FOR THE ARTS

This activity is made possible in part by a grant from the Minnesota State Arts Board, through an appropriation by the Minnesota State Legislature and a grant from the National Endowment for the Arts. MINNESOTA
STATE ARTS BOARD

TARGET.

To you and our many readers across the country,
we send our thanks for your continuing support.

Good books are brewing at coffeehousepress.org